The critics love

Adult Education

"This is an engaging, engrossing, sometimes wallopingly funny novel. Women will see themselves or their best friends; if they don't know Becca, consciousness raised to the threshold of hysteria, then they'll recognize Ulli, carefully restrained to the point of perfection. Men will want to know both women for comparative if not carnal knowledge ... The discovery of Jaffee is a delight."
— *The Los Angeles Times Book Review*

"Miss Jaffee has fluency, energy, comic verve, and a less pinpointable quality of sheer likeableness." — *The New York Times Book Review*

"Fervent and funny ... There's no soft focus, no airbrush. She launches into details about which women are matter-of-fact and men are notoriously squeamish. Becca's water breaks, her breasts leak. Becca behaves, for the most part, the way women do when men aren't watching ... Jaffee deals big blows but always in small scenes. Nothing is inconsequential. The meaning of a given scene never eludes us either, because Jaffee knows exactly what details to record ... The book clips right along — firmly, effectively." — *The Washington Post*

"A sad, funny tale of women's friendship ... the scenes have the ring of surprising truth, of a secret not yet told." — *The Philadelphia Inquirer*

"Annette Williams Jaffee is a conscious stylist. *Adult Education* is sparky, mordant and informed by an ironical awareness of the strengths and limitations of feminist analysis that help the narrative transcend its fashionable theme — the sisterhood of two young women friends in middle class America ... Exuberantly moving, the book brings fresh illumination to the old obsessions by which men and women are united as they are divided — sex and death." — *The London Times Literary Supplement*

"Imaginative, searching ... Jaffee portrays heartbreaking scenes beautifully ... *Adult Education* is a fine, strong work, one that frequently strikes to the heart of the fearful complexities inherent in human relationships." — *The Dallas Morning News*

ADULT EDUCATION

Annette Williams Jaffee

Leapfrog Press
Wellfleet, Massachusetts
www.leapfrogpress.com

The Ontario Review Press hardcover Edition: 1981.
Warner Books Trade Paperback Edition: 1982.
Leapfrog Press Trade Paperback Edition: 2000.
ISBN 0-9654578-9-3

The Library of Congress has catalogued the Ontario Review Hardcover edition as follows:
Jaffee, Annette Williams, 1945–
  Adult Education.
    I. Title.
PS3560.A317A65   813´.54   80-84834
ISBN 0-86538-007-4   AACR2

ACKNOWLEDGMENTS ♦ *Chappell Music Company:* Lyrics from "Sonny Boy" by Jolson,
DeSylva, Brown & Henderson, copyright ©1928 by DeSylva, Brown & Henderson, Inc.
Copyright renewed, assigned to Chappell & Co., Inc. International copyright secured.
All rights reserved. Used by permission. ♦ *Combine Music Corporation:* Lyrics of "Me and
Bobby McGee" by Kris Kristofferson and Fred Foster, copyright ©1969 Combine Music
Corp. Used by permission. ♦ *Frank Music Corp.:* Lyrics of "On a Slow Boat to China" by
Frank Loesser, copyright ©1948 Frank Music Corp., copyright © renewed 1976 Frank
Music Corp. International copyright secured. All rights reserved. Used by permission.
♦ *Edwin H. Morris & Company:* Lyrics from "The Christmas Song (Chestnuts Roasting
on an Open Fire)," lyric & music: Robert Wells & Mel Torme, copyright ©1946 Edwin
H. Morris & Company, A Division of MPL Communications, Inc. International copy-
right secured. All rights reserved. Used by permission. ♦ *United Artists Music:* Lyrics
from "Over the Rainbow" by Harold Arlen and E.Y. Harburg, copyright ©1938, 1939
(renewed 1966, 1967) Metro-Goldwyn-Mayer, Inc. All rights administered and controlled by Leo Feist, Inc. All rights reserved. Used by permission. And lyrics from
"We're Off to See the Wizard" by Harold Arlen and E.Y. Harburg, copyright ©1939,
renewed 1967 Metro-Goldwyn-Mayer, Inc. All rights administered and controlled by
Leo Feist, Inc. All rights reserved. Used by permission. ♦ *Warner Bros. Music:* Lyrics
from "The Times They Are A-Changin'" by Bob Dylan, copyright ©1963 Warner Bros.,
Inc. All rights reserved. Used by permission.

Published in the United States by
Leapfrog Press, P.O. Box 1495, Wellfleet, MA 02667
www.leapfrogpress.com

Distributed in the United States and Canada by
Consortium Book Sales & Distribution, St. Paul, MN 55114

For Dwight and Jonathan and Betsy

"If one could be friendly with women, what a pleasure—the relationship so secret and private compared with relations with men."
                    Virginia Woolf, *A Writer's Diary*

"I will be years gathering up our words,
fishing out letters, snapshots, stains,
leaning my ribs against this durable cloth
to put on the dumb blue blazer of your death."
                    Maxine Kumin, "How It Is"

PART I

One

Becca met Ulli in an Adult Education course in Pre-Columbian Art. They were both pregnant with their first children and sat like two Marimekko pumpkins in a field of withering vines, a group of professors' widows. The widows were off to Mexico when the course ended, with the instructor, who was as brown and round as a Toltec jug. Becca later thought of them during the long winter of her motherhood, imagined their knotty legs in support hose, climbing the Pyramid of the Sun at Teotihuacán, an endless stairway to Paradise, while she shuffled back and forth like a tired obedient cow. She knew from her Lamaze training that Childbirth was the Ultimate Experience, but that winter she sometimes wished she'd gone on the trip instead.

Her water broke on the afternoon of the final class and, consequently, she never learned Ulli's last name. All winter she diligently read the weekly local column beginning, "Fifteen boys and thirteen girls were born in Community Hospital this week . . ." looking for a Swedish surname. Babies were listed under Mr. and Mrs. Father's name, of course, as if they had sneaked in through the emergency entrance and registered at the front desk with only their father's assistance.

In the spring, the instructor gave a party at his house to show the slides from the trip. Plump, still dressed in maternity clothes, Becca recognized Ulli across the dining room. Tall and slim, in a pink linen sheath, Ulli looked as if she had given birth to a feather. Her husband was not Swedish, after all, but John Folger, whom Becca and Gerry watched report the six o'clock news.

"Boy," announced Ulli.

"Girl," Becca replied breathlessly. "My water broke before the last class and . . ."

"Oh, God," moaned Gerry, who taught at the University, "Do I have to hear this . . . ?"

"Like a drink, old man?" asked John.

Ulli and Becca found a corner in the upstairs hallway and, surrounded by little Mayan household gods, armed with a bowl of tortilla chips, a couple of salty wicked margaritas and an ashtray, they got down to facts. As Becca could have guessed, Ulli had merely uncrossed her silky knees and her son Christopher had slid painlessly into this world, whereas Alexandra, Becca's daughter, had fought her entrance for twenty hours, as if to establish her independence from the beginning. Becca's episiotomy had become infected and she still ate every meal sitting on the foam rubber doughnut that Gerry had hurriedly fetched from the pharmacy, along with the bicycle-horn-shaped breast pump, and the tiny manicure scissors and the boxes of pads and other *objets* decorating their lives these days. Early Spock, Becca called the style.

Right on cue, Becca's breasts woke up, as if there were two electric buzzers in her nursing bra. Like a sloppy child, she felt milk spill warmly down the front of her dress. She unbuttoned the dress and gingerly unhooked the little flap, like the window in an Advent calendar. "Shit, that was the last clean thing I owned."

"You are bleeding," Ulli noticed.

"Yes. Groovy. 'Twin rivers of blood and milk/Flow for you, my child. . . .' That's a poem I wrote about two this morning, or yesterday morning, who knows?"

Ulli frowned. "Try *filmjölk*," she said. "Buttermilk."

"Huh? Buttermilk?"

"*Jo*. On your nipples. The acidity is good for it."

"It worked," said Becca, when they met in a photography course the following fall.

"Again?" Ulli tapped Becca's ripe stomach, like a melon, with one manicured finger.

"I figured, since I was into it, the equipment and every-thing . . ." Becca was forever apologizing for her fertility. "And you?"

"I am finished," said Ulli.

Probably all the wrong people have all the children, thought Becca, remembering her messy kitchen. She imag-ined Ulli's life as a spice cabinet, all the pieces sorted neatly into the right shaped and labeled plastic boxes.

Squeezed into a dark booth, twirling film through the tiny slits of a black cylinder, with only their fingertips to guide them, they traded bits of information like children with brown-bag lunches.

Ulli's father was a Swedish count; Becca's father was a Jewish prince.

"Ha! Ha!" said Becca, "he really was. You should have

seen my mother and my grandmother crawling all over the kitchen table trying to feed him. 'Is it okay, Joey?' 'More? More, Yoselle?' "

In April, 1940, while the Nazis danced through Malmö on their way to shoot the Danes, Ulli's grandmother entertained the German high command with an elaborate feast: *gravlax, inlagd sill, fågelbo, Jansson's frestelse.* After dinner, the eldest daughter-in-law, a minor beauty, took the youngest officer upstairs for her dessert. Whether Ulli is the result of this snacking, or merely the daughter of her father, the Count Gustav af Wetterstedt, a weak-minded and walleyed explorer with arctic fantasies, is not known. His seaplane disappeared in 1943.

After the war, there were no reprisals for a nation with a full belly and a collective guilt complex, but Ulli's mother suffered from massive boredom. She went to live in Paris, where she turned her child over to the Sisters of the *Sacre Cœur,* although no one interesting had been Roman Catholic in that family for over two hundred years.

" 'In an old house in Paris / That was covered with vines / Lived twelve little girls in two straight lines,' " Becca quoted from the book she was reading to the uncomprehending Alexy before she had left this evening.

"Ah, Becca, is that what you imagine it was like? Like in *Madeleine?*" laughed Ulli. Someone had bought her the book when she first came to New York.

"Well, wasn't it? What was it like? God, I love it when Hamlet says to Ophelia, 'Get thee to a nunnery!' And your uniform . . . you did wear a uniform?"

"On weekdays we wore gray jumpers with gray smocks over them and gray wool stockings . . . how they itched, Becca, you will never know. On Sundays . . . "

"Shit. I can't get the film through the slots."

"Take it out and start again, Becca."

"On Sundays, Ulli . . . "

"Ah, on Sundays, do you know what we would do? If you were very good during that week, the most holy nuns would take you with them to the slums of Paris, to those dank holes, Becca, so we could clean them. Do you imagine?"

"We ate Chinese food on Sundays," Becca sighed. "I can't do this."

"Let me try."

Becca handed over her much-folded film. "So, did they?"

"What?"

"Shave their heads."

"I do not know. Becca, you will have to rewind the film."

"Didn't you look?"

"Ah, I could have. The walls between our rooms had a space on either end, as in a public lavatory. I could have put the chair on the dresser and climbed on the chair . . . but I did not look. Becca, you cannot turn the light on in here."

"I had nightmares about hairless women as a child," said Becca, turning it off.

Becca had dreamed about the Orthodox women in her grandparents' neighborhood. Becca's hair was red and lush and long and fairly curly and she wished to keep it. Her grandmother Rosie had been a starlet in the Yiddish theatre. Sometimes she would tie on a babushka and, between folding a kreplach and roasting a chicken, would do a *bisel* this and a *bisel* that for Becca. She taught Becca how to cry on demand: put an onion in your bodice. Useful piece of information. Becca's grandfather had been one of the fabulous Schlag Brothers, who had tapdanced his way to a chain of Cadillac agencies when vaudeville died. He taught Becca to sing and dance. Not as useful. Becca's mother and father, who called her "RAbecca!" injected reality into her life with the swiftness of Dr. Goldfine's hypodermic needle dispensing penicillin. They demanded many things from Becca, including clean fingernails, good grades and a maintenance of her virginity.

"Becca! Take the picture out now!" Ulli shouted.

They watched as Alexy, in a new sunsuit, floated darker and darker in the solution, until she disappeared completely. "I'll do it over," sighed Becca.

"So, I come to the United States and work for . . . what is his name? Avidome?"

"Avedon! Richard Avedon, Ulli! Christ, no wonder you can take photographs!"

They pushed matching strollers through the early November frost. Ulli, a protégée of long dark winters, became more introspective every day; Becca sang "Chestnuts roasting on an open fire. . . ."

"No, no, I do not make photographs, Becca, I model for them."

"What did you model?"

"Oh, bathing suits, sweaters, coats."

"Ulli, you make everything sound so exciting," Becca said sarcastically.

"It was not much fun, Becca." They parked their strollers under a tree and sat on a bench. "At first it was wonderful, all those clothes and colors, after the convent. It was like living in the rainbow. But then . . . ah, they cut off my hair, and capped my teeth," she grinned for Becca, "and they wanted me to be called 'Ulli.' Just 'Ulli.' Soon, I feel like a sofa with many slipcovers." She pulled up the collar of her coat. "I was glad when John came."

Becca was balancing her stomach like a fat grocery sack on both knees. "I was once the Wind in a Martha Graham production at Jacob's Pillow. She taught at Bennington years ago. Did you know that?"

Jumping up, Becca streamed around the playground, her long scarf and hair unwinding behind her. She jumped from the swings to the slide, executing a series of tricky if earthbound leaps in a pair of high laced hiking boots. "Not I but the Wind . . ." recited Becca as she danced. Alexy cried out suddenly, and Becca, clutching her big stomach, sank into a pile of leaves. "Oh, whew, Jacob's pillow. Well, Ulli, shall we call this one 'Jacob's Pillow'?"

After their walk, Ulli burned glögg for Becca in a high-sided iron pot in her jewel-box house. A dwarf house, thought Becca, squeezed into a little painted chair with valentine cutouts, chewing sodden raisins blissfully. The fumes were enough to knock her out. Some nights, Becca was so glögged Gerry had to come collect her and stayed to eat rich stews made of prunes and pork and cabbages. She fed Alexy freshly pureed carrots (too fine for that palate!), wrapped her in one of Christopher's hand-washed diapers and rocked her to sleep in an antique cradle.

Ulli and Gerry played chess, and Becca, swathed in a fur coat of Ulli's, curled up in front of the red-white embers and watched John joke with the weatherman on a portable TV. "Snow," Becca whispered before falling asleep.

"God, how do you do all this?" Becca wondered, as she watched Ulli baking fifteen varieties of Christmas cookies. Ulli was cutting heart and crescent shapes; Becca was allowed to paint them with sugary glaze.

"It is not so hard. You overestimate this kind of work, Becca. You do things, too."

"Yeah? What?" Becca waved her hands around the kitchen, cutting through the heavy aroma of ginger, of fat candles squatting in fir pantaloons on copper platters. Polished wooden apples, white candles thin as babies' fingers, paper Swedish flags lay on the other end of the long table.

"You write poetry."

"For some people, writing poetry is like peeing," said Becca.

"You should take that more seriously, Becca."

"Hmmm." Becca painted her thumbnail and licked it off.

"Do you know the story of Martha and Mary in the Bible?" asked Ulli.

"There's no Martha and Mary in my Bible."

"Ah, *jo,* the New Testament. There are two sisters, Mary and Martha, and they have a brother, Lazarus."

"Oh, I've heard of him."

"*Jo?* Well, one day he dies and they are very sad, so they go to their good friend Jesus and ask Him to help them. He tells them to go away, He is busy, but then He goes and brings Lazarus back from the dead."

"Good trick," says Becca.

"*Jo.* With his bandages and shroud, you know . . ."

"I've seen the pictures."

"So. Martha and Mary give a big party to celebrate, and Martha rushes about, polishing the good silver and ironing the best cloth, and cooks a splendid meal, and all this time Mary is sitting at the feet of Jesus, listening to Him."

"A little crush on Jesus, huh?"

"Ah, Becca. And Martha is working very hard in the kitchen, serving food and cooking it, and finally, she becomes a little angry with Mary. And she says to her, 'Look here, Mary! I have been cooking and cleaning all day, and you have been sitting down annointing the feet of Jesus!' And Jesus says, 'Martha, you should follow the example of Mary. You should sit and listen, too. Do not let yourself be too much occupied in the kitchen. The other things are important, too.' "

"Yeah, and then I suppose, Jesus leaps up, clears the table, loads the dishwasher, shakes out the linen cloth . . ."

"They do not tell us that," Ulli laughed.

"Becca, what are you doing on the floor?" Ulli had come over with another load of outgrown baby clothes.

"Oh, Ulli, they don't fit anymore. I can't get them over my

damn heels." Becca was trying to squeeze into a pair of point shoes; the toes poked out like satin pig snouts.

"Becca, everyone's feet are swollen when they are pregnant. You know that."

"I wore these after Alexy was born. I was going to dance for you, Ulli. Remember I was telling you about my dancing?" She took off a shoe and peeked inside.

"You buy them as small as you possibly can so you keep pushing your arch higher and higher." Becca pointed her toes hard.

"It looks very painful, like binding women's feet in China," shuddered Ulli.

"But, Ulli, that's where the beauty is, in the pain. Dancers talk about pain all the time, they trade pain stories. Someone danced with nine broken bones in her foot, someone else with torn calf ligaments. Really. One is in pain almost all the time. Look at my feet," she invited, and gave Ulli a guided tour: the nails on her big toes were permanently cracked and blackened, yellow bumps decorated the other toes like the stones on a cowboy belt, cuts and gouges had healed to smooth scars.

"Now, see how much longer these toes are than normal? You actually develop bone from standing on your toes." Becca stuffed her feet back into the shoes and pulled herself up. "I've seen dancers whose toes are that much longer than normal." She made a wide space with her thumb and index finger.

"That much?" Ulli raised an eyebrow.

Becca nodded and opened a box of shoes, mostly worn, mostly torn. "The shoes have to be just right, not too hard, not too soft. The great dancers, the primas, bang them with hammers, crack them in doors . . . I could never afford that luxury. . . ." She pulled out a pair of faded black shoes. "Maria Tallchief's. She was my idol. Ah, her dying swan." Becca fluttered her arms and hands sideways. "What's the matter, Ulli?"

Ulli was shaking her head. "I do not understand. . . ."

Becca sighed. "Neither does Gerry. He thinks it's ridiculous in a world with inequality and overpopulation." Becca tied the ribbons around her ankles. "But, oh, Ulli, you can't imagine how it feels, it's like flying . . . really, it's the closest thing to it." She lifted herself onto her toes and walked slowly towards Ulli, her arms opening into a wide arc. She leaned on a chair, did some pliés, a relevé. "And the discipline, the pattern, the repetition. It's like a prayer." She bent over in a deep arabesque. "And the audience sees only the satin shoes and the tulle and the feathers, not the blood. That's magic, Ulli."

Becca did a few restrained pirouettes, caught a front view of herself in the kitchen window. "Oh, God, oh, my God." She collapsed against the counter, laughing. "Oh, Ulli, did you ever see *Fantasia,* that Walt Disney salute to high culture? Do you remember those dancing hippos? Those damn pastel hippos? Well . . ." Becca giggled, but tears stood out like bright sequins.

They both listened to Alexy crying upstairs.

Two

"Ah, Becca, every housewife is not Emma Bovary," objected Ulli, mending overalls.

"Oh, yeah? Well, you're wrong, Ulli. I see us as an entire nation of Sleeping Beauties!" Becca kicked a basket of toys. "Look at all this shit! Think of all the items of motherhood: playpens, diaper pins, cribs. They're all symbols of oppression!"

"*Jo,* Becca, but for the child, not for the mother."

"Well, I feel as if I've been condemned to a long prison sentence."

"Ah, you just like to punish yourself."

"Don't turn Freudian on me, Ulli. I've already had therapy, *danke schön.*" Becca had a shrink tucked back in her childhood like one of the Seven Dwarfs. *"Herr Doktor* Sonnenchein. He collected warts and paperweights. Really. He had them all lined up on his desk behind the couch and he would move along during the hour, very orderly, from left to right, cupping his hands over each one. He had it perfectly timed. When he got to the Lalique with the squid, the time was up." Becca, dipping slightly at the waist, demonstrated.

"Why did you have to see him?"

"I was being uncooperative. As I recall, everyone is a little uncooperative at thirteen, but not in my family. I was dirty, too. Physically dirty. I never bathed and I wouldn't use anything when I had my period. I just left a trail of blood everywhere. Made it easy for my mother to follow me around."

"You did not want to grow up."

"I certainly did not. I sucked my thumb until they wired my braces on." Becca stuck it back in her mouth for a minute.

"When I come to this country in fifty-eight, everyone is in analysis. At the first party I go to, a man comes up to me and ask, 'Are you anal or oral?' I think my English is just bad."

"Poor Ulli." Becca clenched her teeth. "Ow!" she cried suddenly.

"What is wrong?"

"Do you have a clean scissors, Ulli?" Becca smiled and checked the time on her watch.

Ulli, not a victim of the same folklore as Becca, presented a pair of Fiskars with bright orange handles.

"Ho, ho, Ulli. That is the first direction on home delivery . . . oooo, the pains are really coming now. What time do you have?"

"It is three fifteen. You had better time the contractions."

"I have. It's six minutes. May I have more coffee, please?"

"You must not eat or drink if you are in labor, Becca."

"Oh, shit, they'll just clean me out anyway." Becca started walking around the sofa. "Five minutes."

"*Gud!* You must go. Shall I call Gerry?"

"He's out of town, Arizona or Atlanta or someplace. The baby isn't due for two weeks, Ulli. It must be indigestion. Or false labor." Becca patted her stomach. "Sit down."

"Becca, you will have the baby here, if you do not leave."

"What's the big hurry?" she whispered. "Last time I was in labor for twenty hours. Please sit down, Ulli. I get scared in the hospital."

"I am calling Mrs. Simon to come stay with Christopher and Alexy. Then I will drive you to the hospital, Becca."

"Nope, I'm not going."

"Becca, please. Call your doctor and tell him to meet us at the hospital. Now."

"Ulli?" Becca croaked hoarsely. "Stay with me?"

"I will stay as long as they will let me," Ulli promised, helping Becca into her coat.

"Well, well, Mrs. Solomon, what are you doing here?" the doctor smiled and dipped his handsome graying head between Becca's bent knees.

"I was just asking myself that," agreed Becca. "Ow! I was in the neighborhood and thought I'd drop in."

"You're not due for two weeks," he scolded.

"I'm sorry," Becca apologized. "I should have swallowed a calendar."

"What?" He lifted his head to look at her; it bobbed like a puppet's face caught in the stage curtain.

"A calendar. So the baby can check the date? It's just a joke. Look, why don't I get dressed and go home and I'll come back in two weeks." She started to get up.

"You're not going anywhere. You're three-fingers dilated. Lie still." He placed his hand flat on her bare stomach and dialed the phone.

Becca stared at a chart of blackened lungs on the wall and swallowed. She knew women died in childbirth; fuck the new statistics, this was Becca, an undefinable entity. She thought of Gerry, eating fried chicken in a Holiday Inn in Phoenix, discussing birth rituals with ten other sociologists, all men. She missed Alexy, waking up now to a strange baby sitter. She could see Ulli's knees and left elbow when the nurse opened the door.

"Take Mrs. Solomon upstairs and prep her," the doctor barked. Then he whispered and made another phone call.

"Are you calling a priest?" Becca asked.

He ignored her. An orderly came in, pushing a wheelchair.

"Okay, Becca, you scoot over . . ."

"I'm not getting in that!" Becca screamed. "I'm not a paraplegic, I'm just pregnant. Pregnancy is not supposed to be a disease, remember? Ulli!" she shouted through the opened door.

"She can't come with you," the nurse said.

"Look, Gerry . . . my husband is out of town. I have the right to have someone with me," said Becca.

"All you hippies are doing Lamaze," sighed the doctor.

Becca was not a hippie, she merely had long hair and dirty feet. She cleared her throat and clutched her stomach. "She must come with me."

"It's impossible, Becca. There's a regulation against it."

"Well, I won't go without her." Becca squatted in the doorway. "Hell, no, we won't go . . . hell, no, we won't go . . ."

Ulli bent down and whispered, "Becca, go with them. I will get to you, I promise."

Becca climbed onto the hard cold bed, the little gown "Open in the front, dear." Some thoughtful husband had left a current issue of *Playboy* in the labor room. Becca removed the centerfold, turned it sideways, trying to discern any relationship between that body and her own.

When she had gone to the hospital to have Alexy, she had been so optimistic and cheerful, so hopeful, smiling at doctors and nurses, telling jokes, seeking praise ("Good girl!" and a pat on a bare thigh), and where had it gotten her?

"Come in," she sniffled to a knock at the door. "Oh, Ulli, thank God!" Becca threw her arms around Ulli's neck. "How did you get up here?"

"I just walked up the back stairs."

"Oh, I thought you told them you were a midwife in Sweden, or disguised yourself as a man, in a beard and a white lab coat. Like Lucy and Ethel."

"Who?"

"Lucille Ricardo and Ethel Mertz, friends and neighbors in the fifties. Ow, ugh, *I Love Lucy.* Shit!" Becca screamed and grabbed Ulli's hand.

"How many minutes?"

"I don't know. They took my watch away."

"Here," said Ulli and unstrapped her thin gold watch. Has your water broken yet?"

Becca shook her head. "Not yet. Hope you brought a crochet hook, Ulli."

"Oh, Ulli, I am so cold." A nurse had raised the top of the bed slightly and placed Becca's feet in the metal stirrups. She was shivering and sweating at the same time.

Ulli pulled off her long socks and put them on Becca's feet, smoothing them over her legs, and wrapped her muffler around Becca's shoulders.

"Ulli, please don't go," Becca whispered. "When I had Alexy they took me away . . . they tied my wrists down to the sides of the bed and wrapped a big belt across my belly, and then they ran me down the halls . . . four women, Ulli, witches with wild hair and no teeth . . . oooo, God." She grabbed Ulli's hand. "Gerry watched me go . . . he let me go, Ulli." She tugged at Ulli's arm. "He told them to take me away." She dug into Ulli's arm and pulled her closer. "He doesn't love me, Ulli," she whispered. "He thinks I'm stupid, and he's not loyal. He's been unfaithful to me and he . . . ugh," she moaned. She put her parched mouth next to Ulli's ear. "I don't remember why I married him . . . I didn't know what to do, ugh, ooo . . . I was in love with something else, I couldn't have . . . it wasn't good for me. Oh, God," Becca shouted suddenly. "This is not what I was promised!"

"By whom, Becca?" Ulli asked. She wiped Becca's brow with a damp cloth, let it pass over her dry lips.

But Becca only cried, "Oh, Ulli, make it stop, it hurts so much. . . ."

"Shh, Becca, don't talk so much."

"Ulli, if I die, I want someone to know this about me. . . ."

"You won't die, Becca, you are having a baby," said Ulli, slightly alarmed.

"I want people to know that my whole life has been like learning to walk. That I just put one foot in front of the other without thinking, and . . . oh, God, Ulli, I want it to stop," she cried.

"Shhh, you are okay. . . ."

"Well, well," said the doctor cheerfully, clapping his hands and pushing the door wide open. "You ready to have a baby, Becca?"

"You shaved, too," Becca noticed idiotically. "Ugh, can't you give me something for this pain?"

"We've been giving you something. You're doing fine. You're a big brave girl, Becca."

"I am not!" Becca screamed.

They wheeled in another bed. "Oh, Ulli, don't let them take me away."

"We're going to the delivery room, dear," the nurse said. Becca clung to Ulli's arm as they moved across the hall. "Don't go, Ulli."

"Becca, they will not let me in there. I have asked them," Ulli said sadly.

"Come on, let's get this show on the road," the doctor said. "I'm going to scrub."

"You are all right, Becca. I will wait here for you," said Ulli and bent down to give her a kiss.

"Goodbye," Becca waved.

"You were terrible," Becca's doctor informed her happily the next morning. He displayed his bandaged wrist. "You kicked me."

"Oh, I'm sorry," said Becca. "Next time I'll keep my ankles crossed."

Becca lay on her bed, listening for the rattling wheels that signaled feeding time at the zoo, preceded by a nurse with a mammoth glass of juice to help her lactate. Becca had not opted for rooming-in this time.

"Rooming-in? But we hardly know each other," she had told the disapproving nurse.

Sometimes she was interrupted by a slightly tipsy Auxiliary lady in her pink apron with yet another flower arrangement from another thrilled relation. Becca's hospital room looked like a supermarket opening. Gerry's flowers, flagrantly out of season, already wilting, sat precariously next to her bed. She had already knocked them over twice.

She wondered if he was still angry with her. Not really angry, he had said: miffed, disappointed with her inability to count, to organize events properly. As for having another daughter, surely an affront to both his Jewish instincts and anthropological training, she had worried; he had merely patted her knees.

"We were planning on more than two children, anyway," he had grinned generously.

"Population Zero," Becca had gasped. It was one of Gerry's favorite causes.

"They don't mean people like us, Becca," he had told her.

Becca dragged her tender body off the bed, and in the mirror she shared with Buffy Reynolds (recovered completely with a fresh hairdo and a new robe), squinted at her own gray face. Tears ran down her pale cheeks. She had always had high color, appeared flushed most of the time; her mother was always putting the back of her hand on Becca's pink forehead. Well, now she was gray, tinged with yellow. Maybe, *Redbook* would consent to Make-Over This Young Mother next month.

Two streams of tears dripped wearily down Becca's dry face. "This was not what I bargained for!" Becca said to the old woman in the mirror. But she could no longer remember what it was she had wanted in the first place.

"Here we are!" Ulli shouted cheerfully through the front door. "I will leave the sled on the terrace, Becca."

Alexy waddled into the apartment. "Mama," she said and punched Becca in the breast with a mittened fist. "Baby!" she called. "Baby!"

"Shh, Alexy, Baby is sleeping," whispered Becca and knelt to unbuckle her little boots.

"Is she jealous?" asked Ulli, undoing Christopher's snowsuit.

"Jealous? She's hardly conscious. That's the only good thing about having them so close together, I guess. God, what possessed me?"

Ulli smiled and hung up some clothes. "Maybe it was not supposed to happen."

"Oh, no, this one was planned. I was so high on

motherhood, so into fertility. . ." The baby began crying in
the other room. "Oh, shit. I wanted to eat first."

"Here are the groceries, Becca. Where shall I put them?"

"Oh, drop them anywhere," sighed Becca. "There's no
room."

Ulli rinsed the breakfast dishes and unpacked the bags.
"No Modess, I got you Kotex."

"Same crap. Want some coffee?"

"Sit. I will make some. We had a very good walk. I think
Alexy will nap a long time." She pulled out some drawers,
looking for coffee filters. "I will make you some lunch and
then we will go."

"Oh, Ulli, thank you. What would I do without you?"

"Becca, you have many friends. And you have Gerry."

"Gerry." Becca swallowed and looked at her empty lap.
"Ulli, when I was in labor, did I say anything weird?"

"Weird?"

"Not weird, I say weird things all the time, I mean . . . did
I say anything about Gerry?"

Ulli listened to the kettle whistling. "I do not think so,"
she answered.

"I mean, you know, when you're in labor . . . women
sometimes talk, and I didn't mean anything." Becca sat
twisting her rings around on her finger. "I feel so guilty
about Gerry," she sighed.

"Guilty?"

"Well, he missed the birth, and he was really looking
forward to it. He worked so hard at Lamaze . . . he was
really better prepared than I was," she giggled. "And that
business about this being a prison. I don't really mean that.
I'm very happy." She drew in a breath. "When I was a little
girl I was terrified of going to prison."

Ulli smiled and poured the coffee.

"Really, I was afraid someone would make a mistake, that

I would be telling the truth and nobody would believe me. My father's a lawyer, you know."

"You did not say anything, Becca," said Ulli.

"Are you sure?"

"I am sure," said Ulli, searching for a can opener.

Three

"And the crazy thing is, I'd been sleeping with him regularly on weekends for months, but on our wedding night, I was terrified! I was got up in this ridiculous two-piece white butterfly-wing outfit, like a see-through shower curtain with lace . . ."

"Finger tips, Becca, don't let the palms touch the dough." Ulli was teaching Becca to make puff pastry.

". . . a gift from my Aunt Esther. What kind of pleasure do you suppose old women get from giving brides sexy underwear? And do you know what my mother said?"

"No, no, Becca, your hands are sweating and will get the dough too wet."

"My mother said it was okay to wear underpants, because

I might be embarrassed Gerry could *see*. Do you think I was conceived through a cotton crotch? Oh, shit, I'll never be able to do this, Ulli."

"*Jo*, you touch the dough too much, Becca," Ulli agreed.

And, in their pottery course, Becca never graduated from pinch pots, while Ulli was seated at the wheel after only three weeks. Ulli glazed her bowls blue and white, filled them with velvety red geraniums and took them to sell at the Craftswomen's Festival.

"Becca, where are your pots?"

"Did you know I flunked pottery at Bennington?" asked Becca.

She was racing around with an abortion petition, Victoria hanging from her back, Alexy clinging to a hand. They were all decorated with buttons, demanding that everyone *Make Love Instead of War, Stop the Bombing Now, Impeach LBJ. Peace on Earth and in Vietnam* read the back of Alexy's T-shirt.

John had brought down a film crew from New York and they shot Victoria, peeking from under an eyelet bonnet, waving a mushy teething biscuit. *Abortion Now* read the sticker on her baby carrier. Gerry's mother on Long Island, Becca's aunties in Chicago, and her parents vacationing at the Broadmoor, all watched the news that night but did not recognize their descendent, who was introduced as part of a larger movement.

"Turn, Becca, turn and keep the racquet back!" Ulli threw tennis balls, like psychedelic snowballs, across the net.

"I can't run and hold my racquet back at the same time," Becca shouted, did a neat pas de bourée, pivoted and slammed the ball into the next court. "Shit!" Becca stopped to catch her breath. "I'll never make it, Ulli." She had weaned Victoria a few weeks ago and was reclaiming her damaged body.

Ulli and Becca were taking a tennis course together. Becca never learned to do more than push the ball around, but Ulli quickly developed a powerful serve, a crashing forehand and an acceptable backhand. Weekend evenings, they played doubles with their husbands, while Alexy and Christopher pushed metal trucks through the grass and threw stones at Tory in her carriage.

As John's partner, Becca stole side glances at him. Like a child who believes that the images on the television screen are really small people who live inside at night, Becca never failed to be amazed by John's daily reincarnation into flesh. There always seemed to be a bit of stardust, maybe it was merely makeup, clinging to his handsome face.

While Becca was looking at John, Ulli and Gerry creamed them every set with aggressive net play. After playing, they sat, sweating and hot, in the sign-up shack, and ate sandwiches of rough paté and drank chilled Austrian wines, while Gerry lectured them about the War.

Gerry taught sociology at the University, and "Sociology," as Gerry never tired of telling Becca, from the day she had met him on the bus to Selma to that evening on the way to the tennis courts, "is the study of the history, development, organization and problems of people living together in social groups." It made him uniquely qualified to discuss the War. His latest theory was that the government's anti-peace movement offensive was really a reaction against feeding-on-demand.

"Huh?" asked Becca, changing a diaper.

"Who is one of the heroes of the Peace Movement? Dr. Spock! And who are both the soldiers and the demonstrators? His children! Okay? . . ."

"Class?" finished Becca.

"Now, this is the first generation to have been fed on demand. No schedules, pick up the crying baby and stick a nipple in his mouth. Right?"

"Ah, Americans," sighed Ulli. "They see history in terms of raising children."

"Child-oriented," John told Ulli, taking a few notes for his program on the back of a napkin.

At seven forty-five, the Good Humor man came and everyone would have an ice cream, except Becca, who was wearing twenty extra pounds of mother-fat like a heavy winter coat. The flavor of the month was Red-White-and-Blueberry.

At home, Becca put the babies to bed, drank some more wine and washed her long hair. Gerry was researching the revival of their much interrupted sex life with the nervous enthusiasm of a graduate student planning his dissertation. Books were piled everywhere, opened with scraps of paper and rubber bands to certain illustrations. Becca felt that, like someone learning to ski in middle age, she would never quite catch on to it.

"I have a weakness for masked men," said Becca, adjusting Christopher's mask on Halloween.

Christopher was a cowboy in jeans and a fringed vest, a dime-store hat and a burnt-cork mustache, but Becca objected to his plastic gun. "He'll have to leave that at home, Ulli."

"Ah, Becca, it is just a toy."

"Ulli, you do not come from a country with a history of violence," Becca lectured. "The myth of the gun-toting cowboy has penetrated every aspect of American society. The myth that every man may have his own weapon and carry out justice as he pleases is a dangerous concept. Quote, misquote, Professor Solomon," she smiled.

Victoria, in her stroller, was an angel. Becca had fastened aluminum foil and cardboard wings to her pajama sleepers and arranged a covered coat-hanger halo to her rather bald head, which she kept pulling off. "No!" she shouted, her first word, learned from her sister, dressed as the devil in red pajamas, and carrying a plastic pitchfork.

"And where is your costume, Becca?" asked Ulli.

"Obviously, I'm going as . . ." Becca whipped off her apron to reveal a new T-shirt, which announced, GOD MUST HAVE A GOOD SENSE OF HUMOR OR SHE WOULDN'T HAVE MADE SO MANY MEN.

"Ah, Becca," laughed Ulli, and produced some aspects of her childhood: paper-moon lanterns with lighted candles on long sticks.

"Ooooh, look at all these masked men," said Becca, ringing her neighbor's doorbell.

"You may have a weakness for men, Becca," Ulli observed as the door opened.

Rebecca loves the cowboys who gallop romantically across the 13″ horizon of Grandpops' television screen every Sunday afternoon. She is in love with them all, but, frankly, Roy Rogers is a married man, the Lone Ranger is somewhat threatening, and Zorro has an accent (although, terrific Ipana teeth), so Becca settles for Hopalong Cassidy, a silver-haired older man with a big white hat.

She names her first puppy, a black cocker spaniel with a white muzzle and paws, Hoppy, and for her sixth birthday, while Becca stands squealing and blindfolded with a big linen handkerchief, Grandpops rides shakily into the dining room on Becca's new Hopalong Cassidy bicycle. It has spurs on the training wheels, fringed saddle bags, and strapped to the left side, is a long black rifle.

Grandpops takes Becca to the circus to see Hopalong Cassidy, just the two of them, Grandpops in his Shriner fez, the tassels dangling dangerously near his special nose, Becca in a bowler hat with long grosgrain streamers. In one gloved hand, she carries cotton candy, in the other, a monkey made of bunny fur, hopping on a stick. They sit in the first row, so Becca may lean over the railing and miss nothing.

Suddenly the lights dim, trumpets flourish, a side door opens, and in a flash of light filtering through the sawdust, as in a Pre-Raphaelite vision of Heaven, comes Hopalong Cassidy himself on his big white horse.

He is coming very close to Becca now (has Grandpops arranged for this, specially?), with his big moon face; slowly he lifts his gigantic white hat from his head in greeting . . . but she cannot really see where his silver hair begins and she is certain the hat is attached to the top of his head, and when he removes it there will be nothing there. Only a hole, a gap from the missing hat, and his brains and all that blood will come pouring out onto her little lap. Becca raises her white-gloved hands to her eyes and begins to scream.

Victoria was screaming: masked men and lighted jack-o'-lanterns and now a terrible face in the doorway.

"Gerry! Take that off!" Becca shouted.

Gerry pulled a rubbery mask of LBJ from his face. "Oh, Tory, baby, Tory, it's me, Daddy, it's Daddy," he said and lifted her out of the stroller and stroked her. "It's me. Look, Daddy."

Becca stared at the piles of foil on the dining room table. "You've been eating all the candy, Gerry. Shit, that's for trick-or-treating."

"What'd ya get?" asked Gerry, poking his nose into Tory's sack, emptying it on the table. "Three Snickers bars. Ummm."

"Do you have an extra Milky Way?" John asked politely.

"Save me a Baby Ruth," Becca called from the kitchen. "They're my favorite."

"Yuck," Gerry shook his head in disbelief. "Baby Ruths, Becca?"

"Except at the movies. I always ate Milk Duds at the movies. Milk Duds, the first feature, Almond Joys, the second."

"I ate Dots," John confided.

"Sugar Babies, every week," Gerry chewed.

Ulli stood in the doorway, sipping wine. "Ah, I shall never catch up. Tonight, I shall dream of jelly fish, of marzipan porkers, of the stork who wears glasses on the Marabou chocolate bars," she sighed.

They stared at her politely and launched into a discussion of fifties' cartoons.

"Becca, come look," called Ulli from the terrace. "Doesn't it look like a Breughel, all the little goblins with their bags and flashlights?"

"More like Bosch," Becca thought. "The Garden of Earthly Delights."

Four

"Shit, more snow," moaned Becca, looking out the window at Ulli's. She had left the stroller outside and it would be soaked, but she didn't get up.

"Ah, Becca, look how beautiful it is," said Ulli, excitedly. "Whenever it snows, I think of when I was a little girl and the man would come with his son to clean the comforters. He would slit them open with a big curved knife and dump all the feathers into big barrels. Some of them would float out, I remember trying to catch them. Once, I climbed into a barrel. It was like sitting in the middle of a cloud. Becca?"

"What?" Becca was not listening. "I hate this stuff!"

"But you must admit our snowman is very nice."

Ulli and Becca had made a snowman in front of Chris-

topher's window while the children were napping. He wore
a beret and a paisley ascot of John's.

"In French, snowman is *bonhomme de neige*," said Ulli.

"*Bonhomme?*" laughed Becca. All he needs is a riding crop
instead of a broom in one hand, and he will look like that
un-*bonhomme*, that snowman, that ice man. . . . "It snowed
for the entire four years I was in college," Becca began her
history.

"Ah, Becca, that is really not possible."

"You've never been to Bennington, Vermont," said
Becca.

Daughter of Chicago, Becca is no stranger to snow, but
there one fought it, sent thick-tongued monsters to push it,
pile it into weary gray monuments. Here, snow is white,
snow is respected, snow is expected, with no apparent
apologies. It snows, they simply say.

Becca derives little pleasure from this *fait*, because her
dance teachers will not allow her to skate or ski. Skating and
skiing break bones, develop the wrong muscles, turn your
turn-out inwards; so Becca plods back and forth through it
in a pair of high hiking boots and a lumberman's jacket.

One day, she pushes through the cold into the lush
steamy heat of the rehearsal barn, point shoes in hand, to
audition for Kaufman and Hart's *You Can't Take It with You*.
Madame has recommended they spend some time doing
Drahma! to perfect their facial expressions and head
movements, and anyway, Becca wants to see Emmett Andrews, the new director, close up and in the flesh. He is
fresh (oh, so fresh, like cheese strudel from Grandma
Rosie's oven) from Harvard and London Rep. Half the
college is in love with him, and the other suspect for not
being so. At faculty meetings, he is passed from one lady
professor to another, a font in the midst of an ageing desert.

Becca squints from the stage; it is hard to see through the

footlights, but there he is: blond and slight with a huge pair of aviator glasses covering most of his perfectly featured face. In his right hand he is carrying a riding crop, his trademark. "Name, please!" he shouts.

"Rebecca Schuman."

"What are you going to do for us, Miss Schuman?"

"Do?" She steps forward, squinting under her raised hands.

"This is a play audition, Miss Schuman. Didn't you prepare a piece to read for us?"

"I'm not an actress, really."

"Oh." He slaps his crop across the other palm. "What are you really, Miss Schuman?"

"I'm a dancer. I thought the part would require . . . I brought my point shoes," she ends limply and raises them like a bunch of carrots. She feels tears building.

"Wait a minute," he says. He walks swiftly down the aisle and, like jumping a tennis net, leaps onto the stage, landing next to Becca.

"Take them off," he orders, leaning on one hip.

"Oh, I don't usually wear glasses. I can't get my contacts in in this weather. . . ." Becca removes them and boldly, imaginatively, pulls the elastic and hairpins out of her hair.

"I meant the clothes."

"You want me to take off my clothes?" Becca asks, getting ready to laugh.

"Yes. I want you to take off all your clothes, Miss Schuman."

"I, ah . . ."

"Oh, shit," he says impatiently, and as if guessing the problem, blows the whistle around his neck and calls, "Take ten!" He turns and faces Becca. "All right. We're alone."

Why am I doing this? Becca is asking herself as she unbuttons her flannel shirt and unzips her jeans. She has leotards on, too, and tears her tights in her haste. For what?

She knows her underwear is a little dirty (although, she had been fairly warned about wearing clean underwear during her childhood) and a safety pin holds together a bra strap. She isn't sure if he meant shoes and socks, too, but bends neatly from the waist and undoes them.

Emmett is walking around her slowly, the judge at a cattle show. Every time he pivots on the heel of his shoe, Becca flinches, waiting for the crop to come down on her. But he flicks it against his own calf.

"Good raw material," he says finally, patting her with one cold hand. "Lots of potential."

Becca feels suddenly relieved and elated. "Oh, thank you," she gushes and gathers up her clothes hastily, as if at the doctor's.

"I've never seen a red twat before," Emmett says loudly as he turns around, and, of course, Becca falls madly in love with him.

Becca is cut after the first round of auditions. She waits for some repercussions from the college; perhaps there is a rule about taking off your clothes in front of a faculty member. No word from Emmett Andrews, either. (Plus a dozen roses and a box of candy.) In fact, no one mentions the incident except for Becca's roommate Gail, who advises her to use a heavy cream on her chapped bottom and thighs.

Finally, one day in ballet class, as she is doing double pirouettes diagonally across the floor, she sees Emmett talking to Madame. His face is broken into a thousand fragments, like the mirrors in a kaleidoscope. Staring at him, Becca forgets to spot and dizzily trips into the wrong corner.

Emmett is pointing with his crop and Madame is pointing with her stick. She cocks her head quizzically and shouts, "Rebecca!" She taps the stick sharply and announces dramatically, "Rebecca! He wants you!"

Becca sticks out her tongue at Gail, grabs her towel off the *barre,* does a deep révérence to Madame, and clomps after the exiting Emmett.

He leads her back to his apartment, the upstairs of an old house near the theatre. It is furnished in refinished pieces of Thonet furniture (which Becca has never seen before) and faded Oriental rugs, ceramic pots of ferns, and two pairs of stained-glass windows with long opened lilies, through which the winter light is streaming.

"I have a very special part for you," he tells Becca, settling her on some plush cushions in front of the fireplace.

Thank you, God, Becca prays, her knees knocking, for letting me be seduced in a dream setting like this, instead of the back seat of a car. On her knees, she turns toward Emmett.

Emmett has other plans for Becca. "I find you amusing," he tells her, pouring some rum into the rosehip tea. "I like your coloring and I think you're a good dancer. Of course, you'll never be able to dance."

"Of course," agrees Becca. Why not?

"You're much too short," he smiles sadly.

"For classical ballet, maybe, for Balanchine, maybe, but I can do modern. . . ."

"Smoke?"

"No, go ahead. . . ."

"You should."

"Oh, you mean pot."

He licks the top of a joint, puts it in his mouth and lights it. "You've never smoked dope before?"

"I'm not sure I should. I mean we can't ski, for godsake."

"Oh, Becca, relax, loosen up. Here." He leans her back against his knees and begins to massage her neck.

"Okay."

"No, no, not like that . . . keep your mouth closed, yes, like thiiis . . . Becca, inhale and keep it in. . . ." Emmett pulls

down the straps on her leotard with the kind of choreo-
graphed gesture she craves. "You're really perspiring,
Becca, don't you think you should take your clothes off?"

What the hell? thinks Becca. He has already seen her
naked, of course (along with half of Bennington), although
she is a little self-conscious now that they are alone.

"Actually," Emmett is saying, helping her untie her shoes,
"you have just the right body for this room. A turn-of-the-
century body, Becca."

"Some classy guy, huh, Ulli? A real purist. Can you imagine
shopping for a body that goes with furniture?" Becca curled
her heavy body on the window seat, listening for the
children, watching it snow.

"Ah, Becca, it is not funny," Ulli said, drawing in a breath.

"Oh? Well, it gets funnier," Becca promised.

"I want you, I want you," Becca groans in her sleep, but she
is not of the generation who asks men to bed.

So she contents herself following him all over the campus,
carrying his script (they are doing *T'is Pity She's a Whore* this
spring), irons his silk shirts, vacuums the rugs, types his
notes. She writes poems to him: "I have been raspberries /
First of the season / Plump, dark, furry things. . . ."

One night, as they are drinking wine in front of the fire,
Emmett pulls an old trunk from a corner. "Becca, look what
I found," he tempts, unlocking the heavy lid.

"Wow! Where did you get this stuff?" Becca fingers piles
of yellowing Victorian corsets, garters, net stockings, boots
with high laces.

"Oh, it came with the house. Do you like them?" he asks
with his cat smile.

"You know I love this kind of thing."

"Why don't you try some on, Becca?" He digs professionally through the underwear. "Here's a good outfit for you."

Emmett helps Becca fasten the tiny hooks and pulls the ribboned laces.

"God, Emmett," Becca blushes. "It's a little obscene, isn't it?"

"Shit!" he stamps his foot. "It's utterly charming on you, but you immediately associate something dirty with it, Becca."

"I'm sorry, Emmett."

"You can get dressed and leave, Becca, if you feel that way."

"No, no, you're right."

"Have I ever really laid a hand on you, Becca?"

"Nope," she agrees, gulping.

"All right. Now let's see. Go sit on the rocker, no . . . more forward, that's good, and throw one leg over the arm, and lift your right arm. . . . Nice, Becca."

Days later, while Becca is applying some makeup Emmett brought home from the theatre, he asks, "You wouldn't mind if I take some pictures, would you?"

"Pictures?"

"Yes, some photographs. You look so, so mignon, Becca, like that."

Mignon? Becca keeps thinking "dirty pictures." She feels a chill, like the draft from an open door, float over her. "I don't know. I think I look kind of silly."

"No, no, you look great, Becca," Emmett assures her, removing the lens cap. "Okay, just like we rehearsed," he directs and shoots.

"Oh, Becca," Emmett asks the following week. "You wouldn't mind if I ask a few friends over tomorrow night to see you dressed up like that?"

"Wuh?" Becca feels a shiver racing up her spine. Or is it Emmett's fingernail?

"I showed some people in Boston the photographs I took

and they wanted . . ."

"You showed some people in Boston the photo-graphs. . . ." Becca repeats slowly.

"Shit, Becca, what do you think I took them for? Mementos? I could have bought the yearbook."

Becca is really shaking, she is too far from the fire. "I can't believe that you showed those pictures . . . to people." She feels very sick and bends over. What kind of people?

"Becca, look, there are a dozen girls out there right now on that little campus who would do anything for me. Anything! Not just pose for a few photographs. If you can't stand it, get out. Just get out!"

Becca's poems grow shorter, grayer. She no longer needs to be on the diet Emmett recommended, she doesn't eat. She catches glimpses of him everywhere, leading an entourage of prospective posers. On the worst days, she thinks of the photographs, imagines them being sold in the Bennington bookstore, or (God forbid!) on a street corner in Chicago. She composes anonymous letters to her lawyer father. "Dear Mr. Schuman, A friend of mine had some—obscene? dirty? mignon?—photographs taken of her, and she is not sure how to proceed. Up until this point, this friend has been exemplary in matters of moral conduct and behavior. Love, your daughter, Rebecca." Impossible!

She must get the photographs, must not allow them to haunt her, follow her path through life, which will surely be the straight and narrow, as soon as . . . But this determina-tion always melts into a desire for Emmett, for the oppor-tunity he affords to be passionate and special and danger-ous. Probably he is just waiting for the perfect moment to make love to her; it is all a test, an exam of the senses. Alone in her room (where the hell is Gail these days?), she practices lascivious poses in a small makeup mirror, prac-tices moaning hoarsely, "Emmett. . . . Emmett. . . ."

She will go to him and find him and tell him she must have those damn pictures . . . no, she will tell him she must have that flicker, that pain, that golden chance. . . .

Becca wades through the slushy mud to his apartment, freshly bathed, heart beating, carrying a bookbag to conceal the photos, carrying love poems, copied on perfumed French paper.

Becca bangs on the front door. "Emmett, let me in," she shouts.

"Who is it?"

"Oh, Emmett, it's me, it's Becca, open the door." Becca gets down on her knees and peeks into the keyhole. "Please, please, let me in. I'll do anything for you, anything, just give me another chance. . . ."

He opens the door a foot. "Get up, Becca, and go home."

Becca peers into the room, into the golden light. On the edge of the plush sofa is . . . Becca looks at the long white back, perfection, a spine of porcelain knobs, flat blond hair just brushing curved white shoulders . . . is it a woman or a man? Emmett is already closing the door.

"Shit, Becca, why don't you go out and get yourself laid?" he asks tiredly.

"I only want you," Becca says to the door hinges.

It is beginning to snow again, little down feathers of snow. Becca looks at her feet and sees she is standing in fifth position. Lifting her bookbag over a shoulder, she slides the front foot behind and curtsies to her imaginary partner. "Yes, of course, I'd love to dance," she whispers, and lifts her arms to fit around his neck. She takes wide gliding waltz steps, elegant twirls and collides with one of her classmates.

"Hey, Becca, aren't you coming?" she says, helping Becca collect the papers blown out of her bag.

"Where?"

"Selma. Look." She turns Becca around so she sees for the first time a row of yellow school buses parked along the street. "We're meeting the group in Boston and we're going to Selma, Becca. Martin Luther King wants us all down in Montgomery."

"Martin Luther King wants me?"

"He wants all of us, Becca. Where have you been?"

Five

"I still love him. I would go with him tomorrow if he rang that doorbell," said Becca. They were knitting, at least Ulli was. Becca's scarf was full of holes.

"He was sick, Becca, you could have been badly hurt," said Ulli. "Did you ever tell Gerry about the photographs?"

"Are you crazy? Oh, brother. Even I know when to keep my mouth shut." She pulled the needle out of the knitting, letting the stitches fall away. "I think about him a lot, though."

"Eat a cookie," suggested Ulli. "And so you meet Gerry." She picked up Becca's fragment of yarn and tried to piece it together.

"On the bus. When I woke up, he was standing over me,

angry as hell because my name wasn't on his fucking passenger list."

When Becca awakens, there is a large agitated man with a clipboard in one hand and a black ballet slipper in the other. He looks like a giant bearded elf, a hobbit, Becca thinks. His hair is even redder than hers.

"Is this your shoe?"

"Don't I look like Cinderella?" asks Becca, feeling better, hoping her breath isn't too stale.

"Are these the only shoes you have?"

"It's a long story," Becca sighs. "Do you want to hear about it?"

"Does it have to do with Brotherhood, Freedom or Peace?" he asks.

"I doubt it," she admits.

"Tell me about it later. Don't you have a bedroll or breakfast or anything?"

"I thought this march was on the American Plan," starts Becca, but he doesn't laugh. "I have money," she says and empties a pile of bills onto the seat.

"Put it away, honey," he says gently and pats her head. "I'll find something for you to eat. Who are you?"

"I'm a stowaway. I'm not on your list."

"It's okay, honey. What's your name?"

"Rebecca. Rebecca Schuman."

"I'm Gerry. Save me a seat."

Gerry brings two tin mugs with red zinger tea and dried milk, some cheese and a couple of granola cookies. He tells Becca he is a graduate student at Harvard, joint soc-anthropology major. He is writing his dissertation on *The Coming of Age on Long Island: The Artifacts of a Jewish-American Boyhood.*

"These cookies are delicious," Becca says gratefully.

"Miriam baked them." He points to a serious girl with

thick braids, who obviously owns Gerry. Miriam is not pleased Gerry is giving away her cookies and comes over, perches on his right thigh.

"Mims, this is Rebecca."

"Becca," she corrects. "Great cookies, Mims."

"Miriam. And there were only four left, Gerry," she whines slightly, but not unpleasantly. "Those cookies were for us."

"Oh, share and share alike," Gerry smiles happily at Becca.

Does this extend to Gerry? she wonders. She likes his eyes, warm and brown with great yellow flecks in them.

He is looking at Becca's feet. "Mims, what size shoes do you wear?"

" 'You are the people who will light a new chapter in the history books of our nation.' " Gerry reads from Martin Luther King's remarks at the beginning of the march four days ago. " 'Walk together, children, don't you get weary and it will lead us to the promised land. And Alabama will be a new Alabama and America will be a new America.' "

As they pull into a field outside Montgomery, Gerry lectures the people on the bus. "Don't talk to people you don't know. Don't answer back. Go straight home after the meeting tonight." He hands out the names of the various Negro churches and houses where they will be put up for the night. "You stick with me, Becca, and for godsake, don't be smart assy with those white men."

"Okay, Gerry," she promises.

Getting off the bus, she hears him behind her, "Jeez, Mims, I had to put her with us. How else would you get your shoes back? Did you think of that?"

Flopping in Miriam's high-topped white sneakers and a pair of Gerry's crusty socks, Becca joins hands with twenty-five thousand people and marches into Montgomery.

As they reach the city limits, there is a sudden downpour, huge sheets of dark rain. Becca raises her face and cries and cries. Emmett and Bennington, and Martin Luther King and Montgomery become connected forever: the impossible dreams.

But Gerry is deeply touched by her emotional outburst and stops, in the rain, to put his arms around her. "Don't worry, Becca, I'll take care of you," he promises.

Becca's parents greet Gerry as the deliverer, the rescuer. They had a long list of fears: blond boys, brown grandchildren, prison cells, dirty sheets, rusting abortion tools, chilly ballet studios, reefer madness, spinsterhood, disgrace.

Gerry also sees himself as the Great Liberator; only he is rescuing Becca from her family.

Grandma Rosie having gone to her just rewards (her just desserts, Becca likes to imagine), Becca drives Gerry out to meet Grandpops at the old men's home he lives at, The Happy Hunting Grounds. He greets them at the door in an old tuxedo, his straw boater, gold-handled cane.

"Grandpops! This is Gerry, and we're going to be married," says Becca, clinging to both his and Gerry's arms.

"Howdy doody, Gary," says Grandpops and makes a quarter appear from behind his ear.

"Gerry, sir. I've heard so much about . . ."

"Me too, me too. Which one is he?" he whispers loudly to Becca. "Come along, come along," he orders, like W. C. Fields.

Striding through the halls, the social director at a Catskills resort, he introduces them to an assortment of old men in various stages of decay. "This is my Becca. And this is her beloved, Larry."

"Gerry," Becca giggles slightly. "Gerry's a graduate student at Harvard."

"Graduate student, huh? How many years you been in

school, Barry?"

"Well, I've been working on my doctorate for about five years, so four years of undergraduate, high school . . ."

"That's all right, nothing wrong with being a late bloomer. I had trouble in school, myself."

"Grandpops," Becca sighs.

"Now, marriage is a great institution, Cary, I myself was married for almost fifty years to the most wonderful woman, Becca's Grandma Rosie, *olov hasholem,* may she rest in peace." He raises his watery eyes to the ceiling. "Could she cook! And did a mighty nice soft-shoe, too. Oh, Becca, I told the boys we'd put on a little show for them . . . a few jokes, a little patter, a little Jolson."

"Grandpops, I don't know, I haven't . . ."

"It'll all come back, like riding a banana, it all comes back."

"Riding a banana?" whispers Gerry.

"You figure that one out, *boitshick,*" smiles Grandpops. "And, Becca, cookie," he reaches into his pleated pants and pulls out a few bills. "You don't have to walk around with patches on your clothes. Buy yourself some new jeans or something. Buy Harry over there a pair, too." He slaps Gerry on the back again.

" 'Climb upon my knee, sonny boy,' " sings Grandpops, and Becca, very delicately (how sharp they have become!), balances on those ancient knees and picks up the mime part right away.

"See? You still have the stuff!" Grandpops says to Becca. "Look, Becca, I have a little fortune cookie for you," he says and passes her a Chinese cookie.

Becca takes it, the two pieces come apart easily (he has stuck them together with chewing gum), and pulls out a slip of paper with her grandfather's shaky handwriting: THIS IS NOT WHAT YOU WERE PROMISED.

"Think about it, Becca," he says.

"Grandpops, what does it mean?"

"Goodbye, my sunshine!" he says, ignoring her. "I love you! And so long!" he says to Gerry. "You come back again, Perry. *Perry*, Becca? What kind of name is that for a Jewish boy?"

"I've always felt a special kinship for the Baby Jesus," Gerry tells Becca as they wander through the rooms of paintings at the Fine Arts. Another firstborn Jewish son, an only child, greeted upon entrance as a miracle in the neighborhood.

"What about Tom Thumb?" asks Becca, staring at this ancient, cross-eyed baby, plugged to Mary's yellowing breast, one hand raised in benediction, as if to signal STOP. "He was an only son, treated as a miracle."

Gerry gives her a sideways look, he is often unsure whether Becca is serious or joking. Becca knows she is many times brighter than Gerry will ever give her credit for.

Out on the Island, Gerry's mother and father fill in the details, bring her up to date, paint the background for Becca. Gerry's plump Sisterhood president mother with leaking eyes and his coughing pharmacist father (Solomon's Sundries) are not quite as rich or ridiculous as Becca's, but she recognizes the genre: ironed underwear and matched sets of things.

Sitting on a plastic-covered chair, Becca eats a piece of home-baked sunshine cake and balances the laminated souvenirs of Gerry's childhood on her bluejeaned lap. One by one, photographs and documents are removed from their permanent positions on the shrine, an unplayed cherry spinet piano. Here are the best-camper certificate, the first driver's license, many diplomas, his first-grade class picture, his Bar Mitzvah portrait: Gerry, silent in a crewcut and tallith, his ears like the handles on the sugar bowl.

"Everybody said he'd grow into them," his mother sighs.

"So who's seen his ears lately?" asks his father.

"What's this?" she asks Gerry, inspecting a paper with Hebrew characters.

"My circumcision certificate."

"Ooooh," Becca giggles. "Is this the foreskin?" she asks, fingering the wax seal.

"Shh, Becca. . . . Come upstairs and I vill show you . . ." Gerry whispers in his best imitation of an evil voice.

But upstairs, Gerry's bedroom, is the main gallery. College pennants, baseball trophies, thick albums of airplane cards line the walls, model airplanes fly from wires attached lovingly to the ceiling. Making love in the lower bunk would be like masturbating at camp, thinks Becca.

"Just like the day Gerry left this house," informs the curator, after knocking tentatively, blushing slightly, wiping her hands on her apron.

Becca finally loses her virginity, *à la mode*, on a lumpy mattress in Gerry's apartment off Putnam Square. A train passed directly by the bedroom windows every hour, and for many years, Becca imagined orgasms to sound like the rumbling of a freight train.

Gerry, who has been interested in this project almost from the moment he met Becca on the bus, seems less sure of himself as the hour approaches.

"Hey, Gerry, ow! That hurts!"

"I'm sorry, Becca, relax. You're much too tense."

"Oh, excuse me." Becca sighs, tries to distract herself by counting the freckles on Gerry's shoulders. Nothing she has read, from *Marjorie Morningstar* to *Fanny Hill,* has prepared her for this. Something is wrong, missing; she imagined pale lights, gauzy vision, candlelight; in fact, darkness. Becca assumed this scene would take place at night. "Hey, hey, hey . . ."

"Are you sure you didn't leave your Tampax in?" Gerry asks.

"Of course, I'm sure. Look, why don't we start over again? Like I'll get dressed and get back on the bus to Selma."

"Ha, ha. Becca, it's just like this the first time."

"I thought you had done this lots before," she says, chewing on a thumbnail.

"Well, I have, but never with anyone so inexperienced before."

"Oh, it's my fault." Why did Gerry grab her this morning when she walked in? She has piles of homework to do. She'll promise to try it again at night. Someday.

"No, Becca, I didn't mean that. Why don't you go get some Vaseline? There's some in the bathroom."

"You know, I hate to admit my mother might be right, but do you think this is really necessary for our relationship?" she says, climbing off the bed.

"Becca," says Gerry, seriously. "It's very, very important. We love each other."

"Oh, yes." Becca wraps a blanket around her, like a disgruntled squaw, and slinks down the hall. One of Gerry's roommates is brushing his teeth. "Oooops," she says, hiding behind the open door.

"Hi, Becca," he grins broadly, lather dripping down his chin.

She cautiously extends a bare arm into the room. "Could you hand me the Vaseline, Barry?"

"Sure, Becca," he smiles, toothpaste exploding from his open mouth. "You lubricating your poetry notes?"

Becca grabs the wide jar and rushes back to Gerry. "You bastard!" she screams, beating him on the back. "You told me nobody was home."

"I thought Barry was sleeping. Jeez, Becca, he doesn't mind." Gerry gets back to work. "Hey, this stuff is wonderful. Becca. Becca?"

Becca thinks of Grandpops at the circus, of the sunlight

streaming through the lily windows at Emmett's house, of his half-moon nails, of . . . "Huh?"

"I love you, Becca."

"I love you, too, Gerry." Becca lies on her back and watches the shifting patterns of the ceiling. She makes out Emmett's white face, his tongue sticking out at her. Becca remembers the cold swift motion as he pulls down the straps on her leotard. "Ow!" she screams.

"Becca?" Gerry whispers. "Are you all right?"

"Did you do it?" she asks, looking down.

"Poor Becca, it will be more fun for you the next time. I promise, I promise," he rubs her slumped shoulders.

What next time? thinks Becca, who is certain no one will persuade her to do this again soon.

"Hey, Becca, look at this!" Gerry points excitedly to a narrow stream of dark blood trickling down the gray sheet. "You know, Becca, in many societies, this sheet is hung ritually out the window."

Becca imagines it flapping out the window, a wild lost ghost, landing on the windshield of the passing train; imagines the engineer's startled face; he had probably not counted on today's domestic disaster.

"Why don't you just take a picture of it, Gerry?" she suggests flippantly and starts to shake. Did I say that? she wonders. She feels she is sinking into the floor and holds desperately onto Gerry, a gesture he mistakes for passion.

Becca is filled with an enormous sadness, not for the removal of a wafer of useless skin, but by the fulfillment of destiny, the pattern of an ancient scheme, the sudden realization that this act will probably lead to marriage.

Six

Becca is counting, which is not her forte. Twenty-eight, twenty-nine, thirty, thirty-one, thirty-two. Oh, God, maybe, she has miscounted. Do you start counting on the first day or the last day? She throws the calendar against the floor and sticks a finger in her panties to check.

From the beginning, Becca has been as regular as, well, her favorite image is the moon; she likes the white shiny goddess aspects, likes sailors setting their course by her, farmers planting their crops. Gerry, that student of birth ritual and data, has, for some reason, given Becca the responsibility for birth control, a topic infrequently discussed in the Schuman house. Never, Becca can recollect.

So here she is, turning into a classic heroine before her

very eyes. She knows about gin and hot baths from reading Doris Lessing, knows they won't work anyway. How can this happen? she wonders, tears in her eyes (Becca cries all the time these days), the one time they don't use anything. One time! Actually, she hates her diaphragm, it still boomerangs across the bathroom in Gerry's apartment. The doctor at the Bennington Health Service, a famous birth control advocate, is always pictured in *Time* tossing handfuls of Enovid to the natives of India, but will not prescribe the Pill for his girls: too dangerous.

His bored receptionist gives Becca the name of a lab and obstetrician in Boston, and Becca obediently fills an empty mayo jar with urine, yellow and steaming. She wraps it carefully with aluminum foil and balances it on top of her point shoes in her ballet bag; she is auditioning for the MFA program at BU that afternoon. In three months, she will graduate. Gerry wants to marry her, anyway. His thesis is finished. Chapel Hill, Ann Arbor, Berkeley: once a week, Gerry dresses in his one suit, stuffs the fragments of his thesis into an old briefcase and flies in and out of Logan Airport like a nervous migratory bird.

An old man sitting next to Becca on the bus peers into her bag, upright on her lap.

"Chicken soup," smiles Becca, lowering her eyelids. "For my Grandpops in the hospital," she lies quickly as the bus swerves past Mass. General.

"Such a nize girl," he sighs, patting her knee thickly.

Becca knows this test is a mere formality. She stood at attention for twenty minutes at the bookstore one afternoon last week, reading the first chapter of Guttmacher: her hard sore breasts turning bluish, her morning sourness, the exhaustion that greets her several times a day and knocks her out flat, the gluttonous eating and vomiting. Oh, the symptoms fit as tidily as her pink tights.

Becca slams the book shut, hides it behind several copies

of *Love with a Harvard Accent,* and wanders next door for a hot fudge sundae. She stares at her blotchy self in the mirrors with the gilded flavors. She cannot have this child. She isn't old enough, she hasn't done anything to deserve this. She isn't sure she even likes Gerry anymore. Gerry will kill her, her parents will kill her. She will never dance.

But she knows she is adjusting to the idea already; looks into carriages with interest, eavesdrops at the grocery store, tries on a big tent dress, wanders through the baby department at Filene's on her way to the lab.

Becca steps out into the early spring sunlight on Tremont Street, pushes her stomach out slightly to get the feeling, and almost walks into Emmett.

"Oh. Emmett," she says and immediately bursts into tears.

"Hello, Becca," he sighs and lifts his sunglasses slightly to view the damage.

"Emmett, can I talk to you? Please." Becca grips the sleeve of his cashmere coat, realizes she has never touched him before.

"Have you had your lunch?" he asks, shaking off her slight embrace.

"Lunch?"

"Come along, Becca."

They walk a fair distance, Becca three paces behind Emmett, so all she can see is the upturned collar of his coat, his neatly styled hair skimming the top, the fringe of his crimson scarf.

At last they enter a small chic French restaurant, downstairs. Emmett is well-known here, an isolated table is found, the waiter immediately brings two balloon goblets with pinkish liquid.

"Kir," Emmett lectures, out of habit. "Champagne or white wine with a soupçon of cassis, drunk mainly in the South of France."

Becca nods and gulps it down.

"Sip wine, Becca," he corrects but seems pleased she hasn't changed. "Becca, take down your hair for me." He helps her with the pins and elastics.

"I won't take off my clothes here," Becca jokes but is slightly afraid.

"Here," repeats Emmett, the adverb forming a bubble on his pursed lips. He runs his fingers through her thick hair. "It's a little dry. What shampoo have you been using?"

"I don't know, whatever's lying around. Baby shampoo."

The waiter slips a plate of escargots in front of Becca.

"What's wrong, Becca? *Escargots bourguignon.* Snails."

"Emmett, I think I'm pregnant."

"Here, your hands are too buttery." Emmett expertly grabs the tweezers and spears a snail for Becca. "Open wide," he instructs. "Do you really think you're pregnant?"

Becca nods, sniffles and chews.

"What are you planning on doing about it?"

"I don't know."

"Oh, Becca, it's ridiculous. You can't have a baby, it'll ruin your body. God, it's terrible to think about those sagging breasts and stretch marks crawling around your belly like thick snakes," he shivers. "I once saw a woman who had a permanent black line running from her navel to her twat. As if I had taken a charcoal pencil and drawn it there."

Becca flinches. Her body is more than an abode, a dancer's body is a tool, an instrument. Who wants to play a warped violin? She has had the opportunity to peruse the bodies of her mother and her friends at the beach, ripply and veiny.

Emmett pulls a thick white card from a leather case, unscrews his fountain pen, scribbles the name of a doctor who can help her. "I'm taking a troupe on a tour of the Soviet countries in June. Get rid of the baby and you can come. You can be my assistant."

Becca lifts her head from the main course, sole, drowning in Calvados and cream, to catch that perfect profile, the corners of his green eyes. Emmett lifts his cigarette holder high in his white teeth, his bow tie is dark green with white fleurs-de-lis. She knows he is lying, he will never take her anywhere, and yet . . . when will she get over the feeling of gratitude that this rare specimen, this exotic butterfly has given her his obscene approval?

Where is Gerry now? Shuffling through the unheated apartment with holey socks, making a tuna sandwich, dropping mayonnaise, the pages of his thesis sticking to the fork, his nails bitten and bleeding, while Becca sits and eats French food with the Devil.

"What else will you do for me?" Becca asks coolly of this foppish character who wishes to part her from her foetus.

"Becca, you know I can never make love to you. But I will find the right partners for you."

Becca sees the wonderfully white bones of that body in his house in Bennington, sees herself whimpering like a punished dog on his porch, and opens her mouth and vomits into Emmett's lap.

"Becca!" he shouts.

"I'm sorry. I never should have eaten the snails. I can't keep anything in my stomach these days," she says happily.

Emmett is dipping linen napkins and handkerchiefs into the water goblets, dabbing and wiping at stains.

"Goodbye, Emmett," says Becca, gathering together her things.

"Check out the dates," she smirked to Ulli, opening the white leather album, which advertised in gold leaf: Rebecca-Gerald.

"Oh, look," Ulli pointed to a picture of Becca feeding Gerry a piece of cake; there was frosting stuck around his mouth and all over the rented striped ascot. Becca's and

Gerry's parents, corsaged, stared with an unusual amount of interest, their mouths opened as if to catch any crumbs which might drop. "Gretel feeds Hansel, eh?"

"More like the Bobbsey Twins Have a Wedding," said Becca, but Ulli missed the reference.

At the last minute, as Becca is standing at the end of the aisle with her parents, her father taps her gloved hand. "Ready, Rebecca?"

She hears the thin whining violin in the distance and gulps. Each parent grips an elbow, firmly, as if she is a reluctant criminal, and they sway down the aisle. Suddenly, Becca catches her breath, for in the blur of familiarity, she thinks she sees Emmett; not completely unreasonable, because Becca, in a final reckless gesture, has mailed him a thick creamy invitation. Maybe, Emmett has flown here to answer why this woman should not be wed to this man. The head turns; it is not Emmett. She sighs, and looks to her father.

"Just remember, Rebecca," her father intones as they walk. "Every man marries his mother."

"Really, Joey," Becca's mother sighs.

Becca stares at her future mother-in-law, a mauve lace matzo ball, weeping under the flowered canopy, and starts to giggle. She cannot stop and pushes her face into her bouquet so no one can see her. She hears one of her aunties whispering, "Isn't that sweet? Becca's crying." But Becca is laughing hysterically, her shoulders are heaving.

"Rebecca," her mother hisses.

"Rebecca, stop this immediately!" her father warns.

"What's the matter, Becca?" asks Gerry.

"Gerald, is Becca all right?" his mother whispers.

The rabbi clears his munificent throat, Grandpops hums under his silk top hat, and Becca, taking a lesson from the Yiddish theatre, and her more recent travels into Emmett's

Theatre of the Absurd, takes a deep breath and swoons into a white satin heap.

"Ah, Becca," Ulli said disapprovingly, "What did you do then?"

"Well, I assume Grandpops called out, 'Is there a doctor in the house?' Of course, there were at least fifteen of them. They probably had a conference and Uncle Bernie decided I needed some sugar. Luckily, *Tante* Fanny goes nowhere without a roll of Lifesavers. Lifesavers, Ulli," Becca raised an eyebrow. "Then everybody was certain I was pregnant."

Of course, Becca is not the only mother-to-be masquerading as a girl graduate this June morning. Hiding behind the Arts building, she lifts the robe to adjust her sagging panty hose. At breakfast this morning, Becca's mother declared no one may graduate in bare legs; Gerry's mother offered a pair of her own panty hose. They are swimming somewhere around Becca's ankles, gathering at her knees.

"Ah!" screams Becca. Emmett, outstretched, is slinking towards her in the grass.

"Hello, Becca," he smiles.

"What are you doing down there, Emmett?"

"I'm looking for a cuff link. See?" he lifts a flapping sleeve.

"Oh, you scared me."

"It appears you didn't take my advice," he frowns.

"No. I'm married now, Emmett," Becca says and, for some reason, blushes.

"I know that, Becca. You . . ."

Becca remembers the invitation and gulps. "Emmett," she says on her hands and knees in the grass. "Emmett, what have you done with those pictures?"

"Pictures?"

"The photographs you took of me."

"There!" He plucks a large gold disc from a dandelion clump and stands. "They're gone, Becca."

"Gone?"

"Yes. I got rid of them ages ago, Becca. They weren't very good, you know," he says, helping her up.

"Oh?" She feels crushed.

"You should see the stuff I'm doing now," he tells her. "Groups."

"Ah, that is a relief," sighed Ulli, and turned on the electric beaters. She was making hollandaise for the asparagus they would eat this evening with ham and potatoes.

"Sometimes I wonder," Becca said, dripping the butter, gradually.

"A little faster."

"You know, the road not taken and all that."

"Ah, Becca, that is ridiculous! You and Gerry are obviously made for each other."

"Where is he?" Becca is running around their apartment.

"Do you think he forgot?" Gerry's father asks timidly, shaking his bald head.

"Maybe, he had an . . . accident," his mother whispers, hardly able to say the word.

"God forbid!" the father shouts.

"What time is it?" His mortarboard and gown are missing from the closet, so he must have left. "He probably forgot he said he'd come back for us. I'm sure he went right to the stadium."

"Who has the tickets?" asks his mother.

"The doctor himself," says his father.

Becca sighs. "You go over to Soldier's Field and wait at the main gate, and I'll go find Gerry and get the tickets. Okay? He may be in his carrel at the library. He said he still had some books to get."

"Don't run, Beccala!" his mother shouts in dismay. "The baby!"

This baby can run, this baby can dance, thinks Becca, squeezing behind the wheel of their old VW. She makes her way slowly through massive Square traffic, cursing Gerry. Isn't this just like him? Tampering with his fans' affections on *the* day of their lives! She leaves the car triple-parked and runs up the wide steps of the library. She runs down the corridor, up to Gerry's carrel. Pushing the door open, without knocking, Becca stumbles over Gerry and Miriam making love on the floor.

"Oh!" Becca screams, her mouth wide open.

"Oh, God," Gerry sighs.

"Turn around, Becca," Miriam orders, very businesslike.

Becca goes into the hall and sits on the chair they moved there so they would have more room. She hears them disentangling themselves, not an easy task in a library carrel, hears grunts and zips.

Probably Gerry has always preferred Miriam, she thinks sadly. She is much more solid and significant with her Mao texts and tie-shoes. Gerry only married Becca out of pity and necessity. She hears Gerry's machine-gun mumbling, Miriam's loud whine; is Miriam crying? Miriam has the qualities of a thick filling stew, while Becca has been playing the role of the Sugar Plum Fairy for many years. Doesn't Grandpops call her his cookie, his cupcake? Maybe Gerry is tired of wandering around a pastry shop in his old socks.

The door opens, Gerry flies out, the sleeves of his gown spread like wings, his flat hat in his hands like a child's birthday offering. He and Becca run down the stairs together, out the doors, into the car. The engine is still warm.

"I can't believe it. I can't believe you did that." Becca is crying.

"Oh, Becca," he grits his teeth. "It was nothing. Just a

celebratory fuck."

"A celebratory fuck?" she asks, unsure of the use of the word.

"Ritualistic, if you prefer. It doesn't really count, after all. I've already slept with Mims two hundred times," he reminds her.

"It doesn't count?"

"Right. It's not like it's someone new. Can you understand the distinction, Becca, or are you too dumb? Christ, a pregnant dancing poet! How did this happen to me?" He pounds on the steering wheel. "Shit, look at this traffic."

Becca is weeping.

"Look, Becca. I went up to get the rest of my books and there was Miriam, waiting for me. She flunked her generals again. And she was crying . . . you know, I can't stand to see women cry." He glares at Becca. "It makes me very uncomfortable. So I patted her shoulder. And then I put my arm around her, and then . . ." he sighs. "It was a symbolic gesture of ending."

"I thought you were supposed to be commencing today," Becca sniffles. Oh, these word games Gerry likes to play! When are they going to get down to living? Celebratory fucks! How many have there been? While Becca has been vomiting and peeing and falling asleep all over the apartment, and feeling guilty about eating lunch with Emmett, this man has been feeling celebratory. She stares at Gerry. His mortarboard is on a terrible angle, but she refuses to fix it.

"Our life is commencing, Becca. Yours, mine, its . . ." he interrupts his list to pat her stomach.

"Didn't you look at your watch? Your parents are hysterical. You know how much this means to them, Gerry."

"I can't wear my watch, because they think I lost my watch, which is why they're buying me a new watch. Oh, Becca, that's funny. Laugh. Smile. I love you." He squints through the tiny windshield and leans on the horn, as they inch across the bridge. "Christ! I'm going to miss the whole fucking ceremony! Five years of my life! Shit, Becca, look, here are the tickets. I'm getting out and walking. You just go park the car and find my parents, okay?"

"Where will you meet us?" Becca watches him disappear over the bridge, hurdling bicycles, cutting through car lanes.

As the traffic begins to move, Becca realizes she could pull into the left lane instead of the right one, could bolt, flee, hit the road. My baby and me. Women do that all the time. Who? There are no role models for disobedient wives hanging on Becca's family tree. Besides, where would she go?

And her in-laws are pacing unhappily outside the main entrance, waiting for Becca so they can see their prince receive his authentication from Harvard University. Becca's parents would have talked their way through the Gates of Heaven, but she knows Gerry's parents will stand there forever and worry, and imagine: the worst! Although the worst has already occurred as far as Becca is concerned.

Becca has made her bed with newly monogrammed Fieldcrest sheets and will lie in it, and lie in it, and probably die in it. She passes quickly into the right lane, the path of no surprises.

Seven

During the rainy season, Ulli brought out her fat picture albums, covered with velvet hides, the pages as transparent as onionskin. Tall, pale people, like the models for Munch's early paintings, stared back at Becca. They posed alone, or in groups, like a birch forest in costumes: loden hunting garb, or long white summer dresses, or military uniforms with high polished boots and shiny sabers. Farther on, they appeared on long, thin skis, or cloaked for the opera. In one shot, they surrounded a huge stuffed swan, with a soup tureen in place of its back, nesting on an immaculately set table.

"Hans, Stefan, Lars," Ulli introduced a series of "uncles," her mother's lovers, like bodies in a foreign galaxy. With each name, her voice became softer and then her shoulders began to shake, her fingers beat a brisk tattoo on one photograph. "He raped me when I was fourteen."

"Oh, Ulli."

"That one. Uncle Lars." Ulli plucked the photo out of the album with a sharp movement and stared at it. "It was at Christmas and I was so happy to be home. And Lars suddenly looked so handsome to me, so big and strong . . . I remember I have never used those words like this before."

It is Christmas and how bright everything is after the soot of Paris. Sweden is like a magical land, the whole world has a frosted look, like the crust of the Christmas fruit, dipped once in egg whites, dipped once in sugar, and left to dry in silver bowls.

How attentive Lars is to Ulli, even Mama notices and is so pleased. He winks at Ulli from his end of the long *Julbord* and passes bits of ham for her, cut specially, down the table. Each afternoon, he lifts her straight up under the arms, his big hands pressing her fresh breasts, to light the candles on the top of the Christmas tree. He gives her a muff to carry skating.

"Take good care of Ulli," says Mama in her furs, as she steps into the car to travel to Stockholm to her lawyers and, perhaps, the opera with Uncle Stefan.

"Ha, ha," agrees Lars, his blue eyes glinting with steel light.

He helps Ulli lace her skates, one hand grasping her calf, the other moving over her bare foot. "Ah," he breathes in mock horror, grabbing the foot. "Nail color, Ulli. Red."

"Oh, Lars, do not tell *Farmor*, please. Genevieve did it, all the girls at the convent do. It is the only thing the nuns do not check."

"The only thing? Your toes?" he asks.

"Yes," says Ulli, seriously, and blushes.

He puts his head back and roars.

How wonderfully Lars skates, he is a dream dancer; they glide many times around the pond. Ulli skates behind him, the heavy skirts *Farmor* considers appropriate flying, her hands in the muff Lars has given her, the ermine tips brushing the cuffs of her jacket.

" *'Ju mer vi are till sammans, till sammans, till sammans, /Ju mer vi are till sammans, ju gladare vi blir. . . .'* " Lars and Ulli sing.

Ulli feels as if she can truly fly, she rushes backwards, soars forward and jumps awkwardly over a log sticking out of the pond, when the pond opens suddenly, and she falls into the icy water.

"Lars!" she screams. The current is stronger than she imagined, although there have been more lectures about cracking ice than fire and brimstone in her Swedish childhood. Lars reaches around her back and pulls her out, lifting her into his arms and skating swiftly back to the house.

"Wait!" Ulli shouts, "My muff . . ."

"What?"

"My muff, Lars, it fell off in the water . . . it is . . ."

"Ulli, it is gone." He stomps through the deep snow and into the empty house.

Ulli buries her head into his shoulder, into the scratchy sweater her mother gave him for Christmas. "I liked it so much," she says in the way of an apology. "I did not mean to lose it."

She is still talking of the muff as he carries her upstairs to her mother's room and strips off her heavy sodden clothing. "I really liked it, Lars."

"I will get you another one, Ulli," he says gruffly and rubs her body with a hard towel from the *bastu,* as rough as the bark of a tree; it leaves long red scratches on her body. He wraps it around her and places her in front of the high tiled stove, as he unties his skates and undresses, also.

"Get into the bed," he orders and she does, although he hands her no gown to wear. Her mother's lies splayed across the wide pillows; one of the maids has arranged it with the waist pinched in, the arms and skirt fanned out, like a waiting woman.

"Drink this. It will warm you," he says, suddenly beside her in the bed. Ulli looks only at his hand, a pattern of gold hairs, like the subtle stitching of his sweater, tries not to look at his body. She takes the flask of *brännvin* from him and tips it back, spilling it on her mother's sheets.

"Take more care, Ulli," he scolds and lies on her.

"Oh, God," said Becca, wrapping her arms around Ulli's shaking shoulders.

"I think it is like a hot sword going through my body. Do you know, Becca? I think pain is hot and sharp, like a knife, sliding through a piece of meat and it falling on two sides."

Becca shuddered. "Why didn't you scream?"

"I suppose I was afraid of my grandmother. She was very strict and I did not want her to know I skated on thin ice."

"Thin ice," snorted Becca.

"*Jo?* Ah, anyway, she was used to noises from that room. I think she did not hear them anymore."

"Then what did you do?"

"I do not remember well. When I awakened I was alone. I went to my room, dressed and went down to supper. It was Thursday, I think, and we had *arter med flask och pannkakor,* as we always do. The next morning Lars went to Stockholm to meet my mother, and I went back to the convent."

"Oh, Ulli, your stories always have such tidy endings."

"*Jo?* I do not even confess this. What would I say? It is like a bad dream. So I take it as indication of my martyrdom."

"Saint Ulli."

"*Jo.* You know, Becca, like the saints in a medieval

painting. There is one I like very much in Spain—Toledo, I think. All the saints are divided into tidy boxes and each martyr carries the tools of his or her own torture, the arrows and the fire. Like a gift."

"Like a bridal bouquet," said Becca.

Eight

Every morning they were together at the Cape, Becca rose early, dressed in a cotton sundress and romantically rode an old bicycle to the middle of town for the newspapers and long loaves of freshly baked bread.

At home, Becca was an impossible riser, a morning whiner, angry resentful and brutish; here, she awakened with the sun coming into the curtainless windows. There was a meadow behind the house, and the neat New England world was divided by narrow panes. Becca's room had one brass hook on the door, and she liked to imagine her life simplified to fit on that hook. One, alone . . . Becca had never used those words before, never craved solitude. Being with Ulli was the best kind of being alone: her tact, her comfort, her long Swedish silences.

Becca braided her hair dreamily in a foggy mirror. She slept alone in a high squat bed in a narrow room with papered dormers. The children were down the hall on foam mattresses on the floor. Ulli slept with her own arms wrapped around herself, a pillow over her head, a tight log of sheet and gown. Around them stood several empty bedrooms, like uninvited guests. It was Ulli's house, rented for the summer. Becca was spending August here, while Gerry did research in Boston.

The men came for the weekends, but for most of the time it was just Becca and Ulli and their children, a pastel community. They ate all their meals on the rambling front veranda off a scruffy wooden table Ulli had dragged from the workshop and scrubbed down with bleach and oil. How simple the weekday life was; the two of them needed no instructions. Ulli cooked because she did that better, Becca sang and told stories to the children. Three small children were no problem for two women; there was a lack of tension, the subtle temptation of nothing to do, nowhere to go.

When Becca returned with the bread, the table had been set with goblets sporting napkins folded as doves, a mustard jar wearing wild flowers. The children sat on the steps in T-shirts, with scrubbed faces.

Becca ate bread and jam, sitting in a woven rocker, her feet on the railing, Tory on her lap. Ulli poured thick mugs with mahogany coffee, supporting clouds of whipped cream.

After breakfast, they packed things and children for the trip to the beach.

The beach was across the street, a rocky beach on a warm bay, private for the few houses on their road, deserted on weekdays. They walked through a short patch of woods, over a Japanese bridge, past bushes heavy with ripening beach plums ("Tiny penises," Becca wrote in her journal), which Ulli said they would pick before they went home, to make jam. Besides children, they carried an umbrella advertising vermouth, thick striped towels, a thermos of juice, water wings and rings, shovels and pails and sifters.

"I feel as if I'm outfitting the Coast Guard," Becca complained. "Someday, I shall walk to the beach with just a notebook, and a small towel worn across my shoulders."

"Becca, did you remember the children's hats?" asked Ulli.

They built a huge sand castle. Ulli was the architect, pulling a Swedish flag out of the basket at the last moment to crown the highest turret. Becca arranged a path of tiny bubble shells, pink as children's fingernails, to the sea. They pulled the children up by their fat wrists and ran with them into the water, the surf tickling their toes. Ulli embroidered a piece of canvas to resemble a Kazak rug. Becca flipped the pages of *Swann's Way,* a copy of which had spent various summers on various beaches, the pages past fifty-three flat and virginal.

By the fifth day, Becca's rash had begun, the mixture of sand and wind and salt too much for her pale freckled skin. She had to hide under a muslin nightgown and a panama hat of John's, and watch Ulli turn the shade of well-oiled teak furniture.

At three, they returned to the house, leaving the heavier items so they could carry the sleepy children. They managed to feed them bits of omelette and yogurt and left them to sleep upstairs, while Ulli prepared their main meal: platters of thick tomatoes floating in oil with fresh basil and chives, inner tubes of tortellinis swimming in cream and butter. Ulli drank Danish beer, Becca allowed herself one glass of wine.

"But Becca I have told you. I met John at a party given by . . . what's his name?"

"Avedon, Ulli." Becca perched on the edge of Tory's high chair, while Ulli blowed dry her long hair.

"No, no, the writer. Mailer. Norman Mailer."

"God, she knows Mailer, too!"

"Sit back, Becca. I remember John walked in, he was big and tanned and wearing jeans, remember this was the fifties, Becca. I think he must be a cowboy."

"He does resemble the Marlboro man."

"*Jo,* but the first thing I notice is he does not talk too much. Ah, Becca, what a relief after those New York writers!"

"He doesn't talk at all unless he has a script."

"That is true. You know, Becca, once, when he was first on television, he was on the late newscast, and the words did not come over the monitor. There was a minute to fill."

"What did he do?" Becca could imagine John's big clear face, his eyes opened like clean windows.

"All he could think of is a story about when he was a boy. One Sunday, in church, the minister said, 'Thou shalt not covet your neighbor's ass.' He thought it was very funny. He could not imagine why someone would want someone else's behind."

That shows you how much John knows, thought Becca, but said, "He said that on television?"

"*Jo.* From then on they make very sure John has a written script."

"Oh, Ulli, did you really know Mailer and Avedon?"

"*Jo.*"

"What a wasted life!"

"What is?"

"This is!"

"Ah, Becca, you do not mean that. I think this is the best life!"

"I don't know. I know that somewhere out there . . . there's something else. Oh, Ulli, I wasn't meant to be buried in the kitchen, I was meant to fly, to dance!" She slid along the floor and did a low tour jeté.

"I think, Becca, the trouble with American women is they marry too young. They need to . . . to screw around a little more before," said Ulli, handing Becca a mirror to see her new hairdo.

"Oh, I shall do that, too," said Becca, making a face at herself. "In case you have forgotten, this is the dawning of the Age of Aquarius."

"We should have them for dinner one night," said Ulli, as they sipped wine on the porch and waved to their immediate neighbors.

"We can't ask them to dinner," Becca retorted. "They're men."

"That I am not so sure of," laughed Ulli. "And they are neighbors. Come, Becca, it would be fun. We'll make a fancy dinner and get dressed up."

"Like Martha and Mary?" Becca shook her head. "I don't know. I don't know what Gerry would say."

"Ah, American marriages. That is ridiculous. You do not have to sleep with them, we will just feed them, Becca."

Ulli planned a wonderful menu: little roasting hens with bacon saddles, their scrawny ankles tied together with sprigs of fresh herbs, a cold velvet soup, a raspberry tart. She and Becca dressed in (Ulli's) silk caftans with long beads.

Their guests arrived punctually, smelling of tropical places, dressed in identical white linen dinner jackets, but over black T-shirts and jeans that fit like caramel poured over apples. They were barefoot and brought a bottle of French champagne tied with tricolor ribbons.

Their names were Todd and Malcolm, and Becca liked them immediately, marveled at their sleek tight bodies and exquisite haircuts. They were very nice to the children.

Malcolm illustrated children's books and promised to send them signed copies of his latest fairy tales for modern children. They had traveled through Scandinavia last summer and knew many of Ulli's place names. "Stockholm is very very beautiful," Todd sighed.

"And very clean," Malcolm assured them.

After dinner, they brought over a portable phonograph and their collection of Frank Sinatra records, and they all danced on the front porch.

"Oh, Becca is a fantastic dancer!" Malcolm said.

"I spent my entire childhood stretched across a *barre*," sighed Becca drunkenly. She had forgotten how much she loved to dance.

"What was Malcolm saying to you at the door?" Ulli yawned and rolled up her sleeves to start the dishes.

"He said if we needed any help with . . . Oh, Ulli, do you suppose they think we're gay, too?"

"But surely, they have seen John and Gerry," said Ulli, confused.

"That must have been what he meant about escaping." Becca was holding her sides and laughing.

"That is not funny, Becca. Gerry will not think it's funny."

"Oh, yes, he will. He doesn't take women seriously enough to be threatened by them." She carried the glasses in from the dining room. "Ulli, do you think women can be happy together?"

"No, not like that. I do not like to think of women loving each other like that, Becca."

"Not just sex. Look how happy we've been together without the men. Then they come with their big feet and big plans and big appetites."

"Ah, Becca, how you talk. You have never lived in a community of women. The strong ones become the men. At the convent, the little nuns from peasant families in la

Bourgogne slaved in the kitchens, while the educated nuns from the wealthy families were the teachers. They were the men. And over them, of course, were the real men, the priests and bishops and cardinals. Ah, the flurry when one saw the polished shoes of Father Antoine disappearing around the corner."

"I hate the way they make us behave like that."

"Ah, Becca, you were even flirting with Malcolm and Todd all night."

"Force of habit," she sighed. "Well, Ulli," she said in a deep voice, putting her arm around Ulli's bent shoulders. "Our first dinner party, dear."

"Becca," Ulli said, disapprovingly. "Dry the silver before it leaves spots."

Ulli did not have to agree, but Becca knew Malcolm was right. This was a kind of honeymoon.

On the weekends, the men came, by various means of transportation, navigators returning to port, expecting heroes' welcomes. First Gerry came on the bus from Boston, then they all made the trip to the airport in Hyannis to collect John. Both men brought dirty laundry and exotic foodstuffs from the capitols of their weekly habitations, and better wine than was available in the local liquor stores. They always ate lobsters on Friday night and drank good wine from slender green bottles, not jugs. They went to bed early.

By Saturday morning, the pace had been shattered. The night before, Gerry announced that, needing exercise, he would walk into town for the bread and papers. He always overslept and *The Times* was sold out when he got there. John desired a large breakfast: eggs and sausages and waffles. He took hours to eat it, it took another hour to clean up, while whiney children were banished upstairs. When they were finally ready to go to the beach, the men were of little help, as they had to carry their sailboat and rigging and sails.

"Why don't you go ask one of the pretty boys over there to help you, Becca?" Gerry smirked, pointing to Malcolm.

"Oh, they won't want to get their hair mussed," warned John, almost knocking Christopher over with a beam.

"Bullies," Ulli sighed.

"I will!" shouted Becca, kicking sand at them, and took Tory and Proust over to Malcolm and Todd's big Japanese umbrella.

By one, Gerry and John were hungry again but would not eat a piece of cheese in the sand; they wanted a real lunch served immediately.

Sundays, it rained all day and the men would glare at them as if they had arranged for the poor weather. They tried playing bridge, but Becca had forgotten how to bid, so John and Gerry and Ulli had a backgammon tournament. Each throw of the dice vibrated in Becca's head. She went to bed early, huddled on the far edge of the small bed, hugging a pillow.

Monday morning, Becca drove an unsmiling Gerry to the bus station; Ulli transferred John to his plane.

"Alle, alle, oxen free!" Becca would shout to Ulli, as she got out of her car. The morning fog would just be lifting. "How do you make it rain on Sundays, Ulli?"

Ulli raised her fine yellow brows towards Heaven, and they joined hands with the children and danced in a big circle.

"Happy as the day when the counselors go away!" sang Becca.

In the evenings they would bring wine and melon down to the beach and watch the sun set. Dressed in jeans and sweaters, the children would play in the sand. Becca and Ulli sat on rocks and stared in wonder at the red sun setting obediently in a pink-streaked sky. They dreamed of separate peaces and places: Ulli's in the past, Becca's in the future.

"This beach is like a French beach," Ulli told Becca. "A beach from an Impressionist painting, a Monet."

"I would like to travel," Becca sighed. "When Gerry gets his leave, we may go to England."

"Someday, we can meet in Sweden, Becca. I will take you to *Farmor*'s castle. And we will visit with my mother. You will like her, she is very charming, very beautiful. Not so much good as a mother, but, ah, history is harder for some people to deal with than for others."

"History has washed us up together on a beach that looks French on the coast of Massachusetts," Becca observed. "Ulli, what are you doing?"

"I am going for a swim. It is such a warm night."

"You know what I'm talking about."

"Ah, Becca, I thought this was the age of Aquarius," teased Ulli through the neck of her sweater. "Try it. There is no one for miles."

Hesitatingly, Becca undressed. She was not sure she wanted Ulli to see her body. Ulli looked like a Nordic goddess, untouched by domestic adventure. "Oh, all right!" Becca pulled off her clothes hastily. "I hate my body!" she cried.

"Why?"

"Would you like a view of the battlefield? This isn't tie-dye, you know," she said, pointing to a web of purple veins on her thighs.

"Ah, Becca, you are so pink and round, a little Degas dancer. But what does it matter if I tell you you are beautiful?" Ulli drew her name in the sand with a shell. "Women only believe what men tell them about their bodies." She stood up and ran towards the water.

They ran back and forth through the bouncing surf, the

waves were never very high here. Becca remembered skinny dipping at camp at night—"chocolate dips" they called them; was it because of the covering of darkness? There was always the faint odor of musty sheets and flannel pj's, of peanut butter and unbrushed teeth. God, the mosquitos, the daily breast-growth checks, the sheer boredom of archery followed by volleyball, followed by softball; the progression of colored swim caps.

She noticed a boat, a white catamaran sailing towards them, three men jumping out to bring it to shore through the rocks. They had moved so quickly, she hadn't had time to cry out for Ulli.

"Well, well, lookey here," a tall overgrown boy grinned and stopped in front of Ulli. "We don't mind a dip, too, huh, boys?" He bent over and dropped his cutoffs, stepping out of them like an awkward child.

"Look at that blond one. Yum, yum," said another, chewing his gum faster and faster.

"Looks good enough to eat," he drawled.

"Oh, boy, look at that red bush! What's hiding in there, sweetheart?"

Becca opened her mouth, but Ulli placed a hand over it. "Shh, put your clothes on, Becca." She picked up her own jeans.

"Aw, you gettin' cold?"

"I'll keep you warm, honey."

"This is a private beach," Ulli said, backing up near Becca so they formed a wall in front of the children. "I will have you arrested."

"Aw, we're just having a little party. Hey, let's have some wine." He lifted the bottle, took a slug, and passed it to his friends.

"Get out of here!" Ulli repeated angrily.

"Oooo la la! Listen to that accent. I hear these foreign girls do something real special," he whispered to the others while they spattered wine.

"Mommy! Mommy!" Alexy cried suddenly, stuck her thumb in her mouth and wound her other hand around Becca's leg.

"Mommy! Mommy!" Christopher mimicked, and dropping his pants, peed on one of the men's feet.

"Hey! Watch that, kid!"

"Oh-oh, Mommy, looka Christoph," giggled Alexy.

Waddling over to the leader, Tory demanded, "Uppyuppy, uppy-uppy, Daddy," and tried to grab his swinging penis.

"Becca, come. Take the children, we will come back for our things later."

"Bastards!" Becca shouted from the safety of the path. "Shmucks!"

"Ah, they are just drunk college boys, Becca," said Ulli, as they hurried along.

"There are a lot of dames your age who'd be grateful for a little action!" one of them shouted after the retreating women.

"Oh, they make me so fucking angry." Becca stormed around the porch. "Well, are you ready to live without men? Ulli? Ulli, are you okay?"

Ulli sat silently on the porch swing, one leg curled up to her chin, the other was sliding over the floor with the smooth swinging motion.

"I am just tired, Becca. I would like to sit alone for a minute. Then I will get up."

"No, no, please, sit down. Wonder Woman is in residence!" Becca said, with a mixture of concern for Ulli and relief at being home. She quickly built a fire in the hibachi, patted hamburgers like clay platters, dressed children in footed pajamas, patted bottoms, recited *Good Night Moon*. She brought Ulli a tray on the porch, where she was still sitting.

"This is what I did not tell you, Becca."

"Hum?"

"About Lars."

Becca stopped rocking; she could hear Ulli's breath through the cricket sounds and rocker creaks.

"The reason I do not confess at the convent is that I . . . I am in love with Lars. I can think of nothing else, only him."

Lars skates through the daydreams of Ulli's convent life: while she is bent over the life of a saint in the icy library, or lying on the pillowless cot, Ulli remembers the pieces she wants to, rethreads them so she can play it back the way she must: his arms as he lifts her from the pond, his breath on her face, the cold skill of his big hands.

Home for the summer, it is Ulli who now looks for Lars, rises early so she may ride with him, squeezes between guests at the long picnic table so she will sit next to him.

"Ah, Lars," says Mama, amused. "Ulli is having her first little crush on *you*."

Lars is not amused, he is threatened, angry; he snaps at Ulli, takes a crop to her pony for no reason. One night, she lets a full pitcher of cream slip through her shaking hands. It crashes next to his bare feet; he slaps her hard across the face.

Listlessly she wanders through the endless Swedish summer days, hunting for Lars. She swings an empty basket for collecting strawberries or mushrooms but is stalking a winter of dreams. Once, she hears voices, her mother's vaguely operatic giggle, Lars' harsh guffaws, peeks through a tangle of white branches to see the dropped curtain of her mother's hair, her mother's blueish-white shoulders. Lars hears Ulli's step, sees her face broken by birches, stares at her through the one eye not hidden by her mother's back, like a Cyclops.

"Lars . . . *was?*" asks Mama.

"Shhh," he commands. "Scat! Scat!" he shouts.

Ulli drops the basket and flies through the woods. But she hears Lars. "Only a frightened little animal," he says in a normal voice. "A rabbit. Or a fox."

"Oh, Ulli," sighed Becca. "What did John say when you told him this?"

"John?" Ulli's voice was loud and firm. "But I have never told John all this, Becca. What would he think of me?"

"But Ulli, John is . . ."

"*Nej*, Becca. There are some things he could never know."

PART II

One

In the supermarket, between the cat food and the spaghetti, Becca caught sight of Madame waddling down the aisle. It must be Madame, because who else is so turned out? And she is leading with her bosom, surely the largest tits in the history of modern dance. They are so big, they even made the girls giggle and whisper that Ted Shawn had . . . during a crucial lift.

Becca was wandering up and down the aisles like a prisoner at Knossos, pushing Tory in the cart, directing Alexy's selection of media-dictated desires, and singlehandedly waging war on the major cereal manufacturers. She was holding open the chapter on healthy snacks in *The New York Times Natural Foods Cookbook,* while gesticulating wildly at Alexy, who was skipping helpfully ahead of her.

"No! Absolutely not! Raisins. You may have raisins. Yes, the little red boxes with the gypsy on the front. What? Gypsies are wanderers, nomads. Raisins are dried grapes. Jesus! Not that granola, it has brown sugar. They should be prosecuted for that. We'll make our own."

So, she steered right into Madame, leading with her breasts and "reflected in more than Oriental splendor."

"Madame!" shouted Becca, almost falling into a deep révérence.

"Rebecca!" rolled Madame. "Rebecca, you are a regular pudding."

Becca signaled with her hands to indicate her daughters, the reason for her current disguise as a dessert.

"Ooooh, but they are little dumplings," cooed Madame, allowing a bejeweled hand to pass over each head in benediction. "Are they dancing?" she asked, sotto voce.

"They're more into finger painting."

"But we must begin some training *tout de suite! En première!*" she snapped and bending over, the gown brushing the tiled floor, turned Alexy's surprised feet out. "Very encouraging," she smiled to Becca.

"But what are you doing here, Madame?"

"I have been asked to develop a course in dance for the University. Now that there will be women here, there must be dance!" She clapped her hands.

"Shit. Isn't that just like them? Shall we teach them mathematics and physics? No, we'll teach them how to sing and dance. 'Women's studies.' "

"Rebecca, it was good enough for you," Madame objected, slightly hurt.

"I thought we were making strides," said Becca, gloomily, discarding a box of Fruity Choco-Chunkies Alexy had sneaked into the cart.

"Now, Rebecca, give me your phone number. I shall call

you when I find out the times of my classes." She swept a hand across Becca. "We must do something for you, before it is too late!"

To an old leotard and a pair of tights, whose crotch did not quite reach hers and hung like a hammock suspended between her two thighs, Becca added a little flounce of a skirt. She did not wish to offend the other students, who were probably unused to such excesses of the body.

Madame, a disciple of Isadora Duncan, began each class with Dalcroze eurythmics. Becca sat cross-legged on the old gym floor, the glory of male sweat captured forever beneath many layers of polyurethane, and clapped out all three of her names, as if it were an elegant football cheer.

She was surprised how much her body remembered and responded to the ancient commands, how the steps of girlhood were not forgotten, how the arm and neck fell into classic position.

En première! En second! En troisième! En quatrième! En cinquième! Cecchetti arm! Cecchetti arm: that long stretch of an upturned arm, the neck pulled sideways, eyes peering to the back heel. Cecchetti, the little Italian who brought dance to icy Russia, who freed the leg, so it could move 360 degrees. *"Ronds de jambe en l'air,"* called Madame.

But where is Gail, always placed behind Becca at the *barre?* And where is Emmett, evil, hunched over his crop and contemplating Becca's juicy thighs? Oh, the life of the body, thought Becca. *Glissades, glissades.*

"Jeté! En tourant!" tapped Madame's new stick.

But Becca's tour jeté was frankly less than flaky, and landed, like the yeasty dough at the local bakery, in front of Madame.

"Well, Rebecca," sighed Madame. "I hope you have kept up your poetry."

*   *   *

Becca was writing poetry these days, in the Women's Poetry Cooperative, an outgrowth of her consciousness-raising group, which had recently disbanded.

"Had they finished consciousness raising?" one woman asked suspiciously.

"How high can it be raised?" another countered.

" 'Raise high the roofbeam, carpenters,' " intoned a former English major. "Carpentresses?" she corrected herself, and was immediately hooted down.

As John Folger had predicted one night on the six o'clock news roundup, it had changed the face of society. "For all time," he said.

There had been six divorces in Becca's group alone, and several women had declared themselves capable of loving other women. One small graying lady in a blue pants suit put her head on Becca's shoulder one evening, much to Becca's discomfort, but she never came back.

In order to free themselves of male images of beauty, they all took their clothes off, dumped them in the middle of the floor, and sat around naked, looking and not looking at each other's bodies.

"What nice breasts you have," they were supposed to say to Lynn, whose breasts sagged like balloons half filled with water.

Or, "Of course, they're just the right size," to Jean, who had tits like two mosquito bites.

And, "Well, they hardly show," to Pat, who had stretch marks like the gouges of a child's boot on a freshly waxed floor.

Becca stared at the smörgåsbord of breasts, rows of pubic hair like swatches of carpet in a sample book, hairy moles and jagged Caesarean scars, stretch marks and varicose veins. The scars of woman-being, the words formed in her head.

At midnight, with a big whoosh of relief, they put out their cigarettes and put on their clothes and went home. No one ever suggested they do it again, and enough damage having been done, the group folded. Sometimes, Becca imagined that was the definition of a raised consciousness: adequate damage.

Becca was also giving a Modern Dance for Mothers class on Monday mornings in the sanctuary of the new Unitarian Church. They danced in front of the Nevelson altarpiece. Becca, who believed everyone can dance, should dance, must dance, encouraged the women to bring their children to class, but they preferred to hire a baby sitter, a pimply graduate student's wife who was five-months pregnant. Her method of child care alternated between tears and shouts, and she asked Becca every week if it was too late for an abortion. Becca had to take her home and fill her with herbal teas and granola cookies and the joys of motherhood.

Ulli was her major disappointment. Ulli, whose only reactions to Becca's CR group were disbelief and amusement, tried the Modern Dance class out of loyalty but could not touch her toes or lift her leg above her knee.

"But, Ulli, this is impossible. Look!" Becca took her own foot in her hand, and handling it like a coddled egg, lifted it smoothly upwards, her knee touching her ear.

"Ah, Becca, mine will not go."

"Nonsense. You're a fantastic athlete, Ulli. My God, you wipe up the courts with me."

"Becca, just because I can do one thing, does not mean I can do the other. And I do not like to go 'ooooom' either."

Becca went "om" on Tuesday and Thursday mornings in the basement of her apartment building. Wrapped in

garments reminding her of the cheesecloth her grandmother draped over the Thanksgiving turkey, Becca sat
straight-faced and cross-legged on an antique prayer rug
Ulli gave her for her birthday, the vibrations of
"oooooooommmmmmmm" tickling the back of her tongue
and front teeth. She was emptying her mind. One morning,
lying in the Fish, Becca remembered the flip of a back dive
when she was eight, the silent slap of the side of the pool as
she hit it, the soft warmth of her blood as it deposited the
corners of her front teeth, pearls, on her thick tongue.

"Oh, Ulli," Becca called her as soon as she got home. "I
went back to when I was eight. Imagine. My guru thinks it's
terrific, that I'm almost at the door of the womb."

"I do not think you will fit," said Ulli. "Come for lunch
and I will make egg salad."

"I can't, I'm going to Guri's for a special prayer session."

"I thought you did not believe in God, Becca," sighed
Ulli.

Guri, Becca's guru, was a formerly plump housewife,
who saw the light while reaching for a cookbook in the
public library.

"Yes, Becca, there was a flash and the book fell off the
shelf and flew open and there stood Krishna in a halo of
illumination on the binding!"

"What did he say?" demanded Becca.

"And Krishna said, 'Don't eat that crap!' "

So Guri had traded in her Le Creuset casseroles and her
Head tennis racquet, punched three holes in each ear and
one in her nose, disposed of her husband, a mild research
engineer, and lived with several disciples in a big house on
the edge of town. There she enjoyed the benefits of a
completely micro diet, prepared by an old Indian woman,
with whom she was writing a guidebook for Arthur From-
mer about where to stay and eat, etc. on your own pilgrim-
age to India.

* * *

"That's super, Becca," John said, watching her execute a perfect split at a dinner party.

"Do you really think so? Frankly, I'm a bit suspicious of a grown woman whose main talent is spreading her legs." She smiled and accepted John's hand to get up.

"No, really. I'm fascinated by yoga and dance and all that stick."

"Shtick," Becca corrected.

"I'm not really that WASPy, Becca," he said pouring some more wine.

"Oh, no, your family was in steerage on the Mayflower, I suppose. I see your name plastered all over coffee cans every time I walk into the fucking supermarket."

"We aren't those Folgers, Becca."

"I don't see my name all over anything except old phonograph records. We aren't those Schumanns, either."

"I grew up on a farm in Missouri. When the farm went under, my father sold shoes in Jefferson City. Some other Folgers went to South America."

"My family tried to tapdance through Auschwitz. It's a different kind of experience, believe me." She patted his arm to be nice.

He reached into his blazer for a notebook. "Would you spell it for me?"

"Shtick? What are you going to do with it?" Becca asked curiously.

"I'm making a collection of Yiddish words."

"No shit?"

"Spell it, please."

"S-h-i-t," she laughed. Gerry shot her warning looks down the table.

"You're a funny girl, Becca," said John, turning his chair so they faced each other, knees touching. He blotted a little wine from Becca's exposed bosom with his finger.

"Woman," she corrected. "Did you always want to be a star?"

"A star?" he pronounced, as if it were another Yiddish word. "No. I never thought about it much. I guess I thought I was going to sell shoes."

Becca slipped a foot out of her sandal and allowed it to balance on his knee. "I was almost a television star," she told him. "I made radio commercials in the late forties, and Grandpops was going to put them on television. 'I'm little Becca Schuman and my Grandpops sells Cadillacs right down the street,' " she lisped for John.

" 'I'm gonna get you on a slow boat to China . . .' " croons Grandpops to Becca as they sail through the Loop in his big black car. Becca leans against the front seat, soft and gray as the breast of a pigeon, against Grandma Rosie's sealskin coat, saturated with Nuit de Noël. In the back seat ride Becca's matching *tantes,* also in sealskin, identified by the monograms of silk forget-me-nots on the slippery linings; jeweled and veiled and hidden behind a smokescreen from lipstick-tipped Pall Malls. The good fairies.

" '. . . all to myself alone,' " finishes Grandpops.

Becca's parents, the outcasts Joey and Judith, confined to their year-old two-tone gray Oldsmobile, ride listlessly behind them. They are all riding to the radio studio where Becca will record another commercial for Grandpops, in full view of her adoring family. And Grandpops has a surprise for Becca.

"A new puppy?"

"Better than a puppy."

There is nothing better than a puppy, but Becca asks politely, "A new dolly?"

"Better than a dolly, Becca."

Becca, who is not too hot on dollies, knows there will be

one anyway. Mr. Bennett from the advertising agency always has a new doll for Becca. And sure enough, as they enter the chewing-gum building ("Smell the spearmint?" asks Grandpops each and every time), there is Mr. Bennett clutching Bonnie Braids, Dick Tracy's new daughter, in one bent arm. Becca already has Bonnie Braids, Grandpops bought her one last week, but she has already pulled the braids all the way out of the two holes on top of her head.

The family holds its breath to see what Becca will say, but she says, "I like your sunset, Mr. Bennett," and pulls on his painted tie. He blushes and they all laugh in relief.

"What's the big surprise, Grandpops?"

"Mr. Bennett's going to put you on television, Becca!"

"Ah . . . Mr. Schuman . . ."

"But it didn't work out," Becca told John. "I had the wrong face."

"The wrong face!" shouts Grandpops in disbelief.

"The wrong face," echo the aunties.

"This gorgeous face is wrong?" groans Grandpops hoarsely, and clutching his chest, begins to fall straight back. "Quick! Quick! Rosie, Estelle, Esther, Fanny!" They gather around him, spreading their arms like a fur hoop, and catch him as he falls. "Please, God, I did not hear right."

"Ah, but, Mr. Schuman, uh," says Mr. Bennett, truly upset, wringing his hands. "Becca is . . . My agency has conducted a market survey on the face of the fifties, sir, and well, we find that Becca, ah, looks too much like Shirley Temple, Mr. Schuman, sir."

"Shirley Temple. Shirley Temple! You bet your sweet petuties, Mr. Bennett, she looks like Shirley Temple. But with RED curls! Right, girls?"

"Shirley Temple!" the aunties exhale in unison, like the Andrews Sisters.

"Well. Shirley Temple, Mr. Schuman, is outdated, passé, not a fifties image."

Grandpops takes Becca's face between the fingers of one hand and squeezes it. "This face is out of date? This face is passé? A gorgeous *ponim* like this? AaaaaaH!" he screams. *"Oi, gevald!* Get me out of here. Before I do something I am sorry for!"

"The voice is okay, Mr. Schuman," says Mr. Bennett, following the hustling entourage down the corridor to the bank of elevators. "It's a great little voice. We could dub it with another face."

"Another face?" shouts Grandpops in disbelief. "No face, no voice!" he says as they descend.

"Whose face did they use?"

"Oh, they got Nellie Fox of the White Sox. He had the right face, evidently." She sighed. "I miss my fan club."

"Let's dance," said John.

Becca wound an arm around John's neck. He was a big man; she had never danced with him before. She was leading for a change.

John put his nose into her left temple and placed a hand on her rump. "Ummm, what a lovely tail you have, Becca."

Becca forgot about the women's movement for a minute. "We specialize in those. You know how the Eskimos have two hundred words for snow, in my family we have the same number of words for bottoms. Tushy, bottom, buns, bummy," Becca named a few of the less exotic ones for him. "I even have an Aunt Fanny." They twirled around the room. Ulli and Gerry were dancing together. " 'Thou shalt not covet thy neighbor's ass,' John!"

"Oh, God, Becca, did you see me do that?" John asked, horrified.

"No," laughed Becca. "Ulli told me about it. Hey, John, you're blushing." Becca put her hand on his cheek. "Don't worry, you definitely have the right face."

That night, while they were making love, Becca noticed that Gerry kept his left hand on the side of her head, and she always pressed her right hand to his back. When Gerry fell asleep, she jumped up (like George Sand, she hoped) and wrote a poem. It began: "You keep your hand on my face,/ I keep mine on your back,/ For each of us drives a riderless horse/Into the Eye of the Storm./I am taking this trip dangerously alone. . . ."

"Aw, Becca, do you really come alone?" asked Gerry, when she showed him her poem. "I thought I did that to you."

"Oh, Gerry," said Becca, kindly. "You taught me how to come alone."

It was this poem, along with four others, that provided entrance to Angus MacMillan's poetry class at the New School the following fall.

Two

The first week of classes, Mac singled Becca out from all the other housewives, actresses, waitresses, and dropouts in the class. She felt the way she had in the first grade.

There is a magic show at Becca's school, and the magician, a glowering giant of a man in a slippery black cape with a red lining, sneers into the audience and challenges, "Does anybody have a rrrring?"

Rebecca has a ring, a heart-shaped garnet in a little gold band, a gift from Grandpops. Winding it around and around her finger, she balances the desire to go up onto that stage and the fear of having to tell her Mother how she lost it. Surely the magician will lose it, make it disappear, will change things for all times. But the lights are hot and golden, the magician's smile is wide and curving, and Becca raises her hand and marches onto the stage.

Becca was ripe for this. There was a major sexual revolution going on and she had just had an IUD inserted; it was a gigantic ring of steel, tricky as a Chinese puzzle.

"There," said Becca's gynecologist to her ass, as he made the final twist, a plumber inserting a new washer. "You're safe. You can screw the entire telephone company on your way home without a worry."

But Becca wanted only Angus MacMillan, wanted his tall body creaking like a silver stick, wanted his New England boyhood, wanted his slim cool hands, shaking always from drink or lack of it, wanted his rhymes. Maybe the rhymes will seep in. Isn't he, after all, the poet who compared the flow of semen to the movement of the waves?

Mac was not really interested in sex. He was mainly concerned with finding someone to carry his bookbag from his office to his classroom, someone to sit at his custom-made sandals. He was a classically impotent alcoholic with a functioning wife of many years' service, and he found the hot women in his classes difficult to handle. Never was he offered so much trembling flesh as he was in those years.

"Poetry is not therapy," he began the first class, but nobody believed him. Hadn't he heard of confessional poetry? they wondered out loud.

Becca was truly desirable, if he had had the energy. Exercise had carved out the original slopes and valleys of her body and he liked to stroke the hill of a breast or feel her warm breath next to his ear. Her poems weren't too bad, either.

They often sat in his airless office in the middle of Manhattan, Mac in his captain's chair with the Harvard emblem, Becca on his lap, her arms wrapped carefully around his sinewy neck, while he read her poems. Once, he lifted her T-shirt and took one of her breasts into his mouth. Only once.

They would leave the office and find a bar, just opening for the day.

"Don't you know who this man is?" demanded Becca of the snotty bartender. "This is a famous man!"

"Becca, Becca, stop it," Mac said tiredly. "Let's go sit down. Becca," he said limply, "I'm famous to you, dear. But I'm like a frog in a puddle . . . a puddle in the ocean of the world. When will you see this? A puddle of whiskey," he added.

"Stop it. Oh, God, don't."

Tears were slipping down his face. "I'm quickly becoming an artifact. 'Oh, look, there's Angus MacMillan, the poet who drank with Auden. Oh, Angus MacMillan, the poet who drank with Dylan Thomas, oh, Angus MacMillan, the poet who drank with . . . Becca, dear heart, don't have another."

Becca caught his tears in her cupped hands. She blew into his ear as if it were life she was giving him.

"This is ridiculous. You shouldn't be here, sitting in a dump with an old drunk. Go home, Becca, to your little girls."

"You've given me so much," Becca said. "You've let me believe in myself as a poet."

"You are a poet, Becca, you will be a poet. Buy me another drink, dear girl." He tossed a folded bill across the wet table.

"Don't try to keep up with me, Becca, you'll get sick. I've been practicing for years." He threw back the whiskey and sipped the beer. "This is not the secret, you know. This stuff, this poison. It neither fans the flames, nor puts them out. It just keeps me vertical."

"But if I read . . ."

"Oh, you really think I'm keeping some secret from you, some trick, some abracadabra. That poems are a kind of puzzle. Russian dolls fitting into each other?"

"Oh, yes! Yes!" said Becca, who thought that exactly.

"And I have the key, the little golden key? Oh, dear, Becca, if I had the key, it is missing, lost, rusting in this tub of shit I call my life. Can I tell you how much I hate it . . . the power? When one is empty, the space, the hollow aches, and when one is full, the pounding is too much for the human soul."

"I want that feeling!" Becca insisted.

Mac smirked. "Anyway, if I had the key, why would I give it to you? Oh, Becca, don't go away. I would give it to you, dear love. But you don't really want the magic potion. Don't you remember your fairy tales, Becca? How, when one finally has the goose that lays the golden eggs, one is in a great hurry to be rid of it?" He sighed. "You're still going to sleep reading fairy stories."

"Goddamn it, I am not a little girl!"

"Oh, you are, you are a little girl, making the classic search. You aren't ready for men, Becca. You're playing house out there in the suburbs. You've found yourself a little boy, a brother, maybe. You don't want men. . . ."

"How the shit do you know what I want? I want to fly! I want to soar! I came within this close to throwing away my life for a moment of passion!"

"Passion," Mac sighed, for he knows all about Emmett, had sopped up her whole life with an old handkerchief in his office one afternoon. "But you didn't, Becca. And you choose to sit in this hotbed of sexuality with old Angus MacMillan, who couldn't get it up if Helen of Troy came sailing in here on a wave of beer foam." He started coughing. " 'The art of our necessities is strange / That can make vile things precious.' Lear, dear." He took her hand again. "Oh, Rebecca, where is the beauty in climbing into bed with a stranger? A sudden love of the unknown? You who have cleverly engineered a life of the familiar? Suddenly, you women will all go climb Everest because it is there?"

"No one is going to tell us what we may or may not climb anymore. We may climb whole mountain ranges!"

"Ah, the multiple orgasm. Major discovery of the women's movement. Always makes me think of a goddamn five-course dinner."

"I said that."

"What?"

"I compared it to a Chinese banquet in one of my poems."

"So, you did. It is yours. See, now I'm stealing from you, dear Becca," he laughed. "And the rediscovery of the clitoris, the lightswitch of women. Another of your metaphors, I recall. Do you really view yourself as a lightswitch, Becca? That you can be turned on and off with the flick of a finger?" He finished off his beer. "Where do you think your sex really is? In your head, in your heart?" His head dropped onto his bent arms on the table. "Where do you itch the most, dear heart?" he asked, before falling asleep.

"I'm in love with Angus MacMillan," Becca told Ulli one afternoon when she came to pick up her daughters.

Ulli sighed and folded one of Christopher's shirts. "I do not want to hear about it, Becca."

"Ulli . . ."

"You are in a great hurry to punish yourself." She shook her head.

"I thought you didn't read Freud, Ulli."

"I do not need Freud for this, Becca. Do you sleep with him?"

"Not yet. . . . It is not the reality of the passion, but the suggestion of the passion that is essential to the poet," she informed Ulli.

"Did he say that?"

"No, I made it up. He likes my poems."

"So do I. But that is not enough?"

"Oh, it's a new freedom, the freedom to fuck. People eat when they want to, they sleep when they want to, they fuck . . ."

"I beg your pardon, Becca, but you do not eat when you want to. You fix the meals around Gerry's schedule. And you do not sleep late, either, you are up with the girls." Ulli was chopping scallions with a lethal looking knife. "What is the matter with Gerry?"

"There's nothing the matter with Gerry. It's just . . . It's the Baskin-Robbins theory of sex, Ulli. You eat vanilla all your life, you want to try a little chocolate."

"I think you are headed for Rocky Road."

"Oh, that's very funny, Ulli," Becca said appreciatively. "Hey, what are you cooking?"

"Chinese. I am taking the course at the Adult School."

"Oh, Ulli, I am truly hurt. You're taking a course without me."

"You do not want to cook. You are too busy being self-destructive."

"Thanks a heap, Ulli."

"Ah, Becca, I did not mean . . ."

"You don't know a shit about contemporary American life!" Becca shouted, pulling away from Ulli. "Alexy! Tory! Get down here immediately! We have to go!"

"Becca, stop this . . ."

"Let go of me, Ulli. I don't know why I've put up with your disapproval all these years!"

"What would you like me to say? Do you need my blessing? Ah, you cannot even go out and have a nice love affair."

"Hurry up," Becca shouted at her daughters, finding shoes in a basket on the front porch.

"I don't wanna go," whined Alexy. "I want to play with Christoph."

"Go away, bad Mommy," shouted Tory, pounding at Becca with a wooden hammer.

"Shut up, both of you!" she said, grabbing Tory's wrist.

"Poor Becca," said Ulli, watching her. "I have lived through real tragedy, you must manufacture your own."

"Well, don't worry, Ulli!" said Becca, slamming the door. " 'The times, they are a-changin'!' "

Becca and Ulli, on the way to each other's houses, passed in their cars fifteen minutes later.

"Oh, Ulli, I'm sorry," said Becca, tearfully, leaning out the window.

"I am sorry, too, Becca."

"Hey, lady!" shouted the driver of the car behind Becca's, slamming on his brakes. "Pull over!"

"Fuck you," Becca mouthed into the rear-view mirror and gave him the finger.

"Ah, Becca," said Ulli. "I think we should move over."

They parked across from a small playground.

"Someday, it will be a policeman," warned Ulli, after they had hugged and apologized and Becca had wept a little.

"Did you ever notice how 'Fuck you' and 'I love you' look almost the same in a rear-view mirror?"

"Becca, why can't you be happy?" asked Ulli, seriously.

"I don't know. I just have a feeling," Becca said looking around the small playground. "There must be something more than this." She shrugged and pushed Tory in a swing. "Oh, fuck them all!"

"Ah, Becca," sighed Ulli, patting her arm. "Even you will never be able to do that."

"I want to put something in your mouth," whispered Becca, fiercely, to Mac, unpacking an enormous picnic hamper at the Peace Rally in the Sheep Meadow of Central Park. Mac was reading along with Grace Paley and some others.

"But, darling girl, you already have," chuckled Mac. He

was in a wonderful mood, uncorking bottles of wine, waving to friends.

Mac's wife, Sylvie, a social worker for the city, sat on a far corner of an Indian bedspread and knitted a complicated ski sweater for Mac to wear in their farmhouse in Vermont. Their teenaged daughters took immediate charge of Becca's small ones and disappeared to row them around the park. "Make sure they're wearing life vests!" shouted Sylvie.

"They don't have life vests in Central Park," Gerry told her.

"Don't let Tory lean out of the boat," Becca warned Alexy.

Sitting under a tree, Gerry questioned Mac about Becca's abilities. Mac mentioned her style, her fluency, her fluidity. Who can be sure he was talking about her poetry?

"Of course, I've always encouraged Becca," Gerry confided. "I personally think she should write domestic poetry. Poems about the girls and motherhood. Visions from the kitchen sink. You know, like Phyllis McGinley."

"Who?" asked Mac.

"I believe she's a well-known poetess," Gerry answered, surprised. "I think there's a big market for that kind of stuff."

Becca arranged platters of cheese and breads, slices of paper-thin prosciutto, a bowl overflowing with fresh fruit. "I have been raspberries: tart, plump, juicy things," recited Becca, quoting herself.

"As white and creamy as Becca's thighs," said Mac, to please her, but didn't cut the chevre.

"Bleeding with the passion of tiny suns," mused Becca, presenting a carton of deviled eggs. "Mac, you aren't eating."

"I will, dear heart, I will. Oh, there's . . ." he said, getting up and wandering off.

"He can't eat that rich food, Becca," said Sylvie. "It isn't good for him. He's on a very strict diet, Becca, plus a regime of vitamin B shots . . ."

"I didn't know . . ."

"Of course not, how would you know? None of you ever knows. He's an alcoholic, Becca, an alcoholic. It's not an affectation, it's a disease. I have to watch everything he eats very closely. . . ."

"Rebecca," Mac called. "Come over here so I can introduce you to some people."

"So this is the latest one?" asked the man he was talking with.

Oh, thought Becca, I seem to be part of a long poetic tradition.

Sylvie turned to Gerry, her needles clicking away. "Well, what do you think of my husband and Becca?"

"Ha?"

"Of course, I'm used to it. It's practically *de rigueur* around here." She looked up from the sweater for a minute. "But I was wondering what you thought of it."

" 'The times they are a-changin', ' " he whistled through his teeth and patted the woman's bent shoulder.

Three

"What are these?" Gerry demanded in a quiet cold voice one night, while Becca was doing the dishes.

She squinted through the suds, knocked over the cleanser, recognized a file tied ridiculously with red satin ribbons. "Those are my new poems."

"Hmm," he sucked on his lip. "I know that."

"Did you read them?"

"Hmmm."

"What did you think of them?"

"I think they stink."

"Oh, yes?" She was interested, but a little frightened. She hadn't noticed how big Gerry was for a long time.

"They're love poems to Mac."

Becca sighed; it was not really true. Mac merely served as a means to objectify certain feelings. She felt the poems dealt with passion and fear, growing and changing. They had as much to do with Gerry and Ulli and her children as Mac. They . . . She started to explain to Gerry.

"Forget it," said Gerry. "I know you've been fucking that old man all year. Boy, was I dumb to let you go into New York and take that course."

"Let me?"

"Here are your lousy poems," he said and threw the folder on the soapy counter.

"You bastard!" she screamed, grabbing them. She took hold of the collar of his shirt and pulled hard. It came off with a terrible "psst," like one of the costumes in Grandpops' old trunk. She started to laugh.

Gerry reached out and knocked her to the floor with his fist. "Don't touch me, Becca!"

"Now, wait a minute, buddy, nobody lets me or doesn't let me do things. I decide for myself."

"That'll come in handy when you're alone."

"Look, you went into my desk and took these out of a drawer without asking me."

"You've been keeping secrets from me for years, Becca."

"Secrets, what secrets? I'm talking about privacy . . . I hope we have privacy in this house."

"Don't play word games with me, whore."

"What did you call me?"

"Whore! Whore!"

"Keep your voice down. You'll wake . . ."

"God, I should have known you'd never change!"

"What are you talking about?"

"Oh, Becca, what I could do to you. I could divorce you and take those little girls away from you forever and ever."

"For what?" For writing poetry? For keeping secrets? "I need secrets. I can't write poetry without secrets."

"Poetry! Bullshit! I'm not talking about poetry!" Gerry shouted and stomped out of the house, slamming the front door.

Becca stood in the hallway with her damp poems. What had she done? What was he talking about? She tried to remember how the evening had begun. What had she done? Nothing had happened, if "happened" was in the bloody-sheet category. Could a person be divorced for keeping secrets or writing poetry? They were back in the third grade or the twelfth century.

She was starting to feel less brave, more frightened and teary. She dialed Ulli's number. "Ulli?" Becca asked thickly, her voice full of tears.

"Ah, Becca." Ulli drew a deep breath.

"Is Gerry there?" Becca asked.

"*Jo*," then Ulli shouted gaily to the men, "It is Mary Harrison, from Christopher's school. I will be just a minute."

"Oh Ulli, I'm so scared. What am I going to do?" Her teeth were chattering.

"What is going on, Becca?"

"I don't know. Gerry found some poems I wrote to Mac, but they're not really about Mac, they're just poems. Oh, God, Ulli . . ."

"Ah, Becca." Ulli clucked her tongue.

"Don't tell me, 'I told you so,' Ulli, please. . . ."

"I did not say that."

"Oh, I feel so so scared. Please come over here, please."

"I do not think I can, Becca. Tomorrow . . ."

"Tomorrow!" Becca screamed. "Oh, Ulli, I won't last the night. . . ."

"*Jo*, you will, drink some brandy. Tomorrow, after you take the girls to school, you will come."

"Oh, the girls, God, Ulli, Gerry says he's going to take them away from me. Can he do that, Ulli? Please, please, come here, Ulli. . . ." Becca was sobbing on the phone.

"No, Becca, I can not. I must get off the phone. You must think hard. I will see what I can do for you, Becca." Ulli hung up.

"Gerry?" Lying in bed with the cognac bottle, Becca heard the front-door lock turn, heard shuffling up the stairs. "Gerry?"

His study door slammed. "Gerry!" she called and got out of bed. She banged on the door. "Gerry!"

"Get away from me, Becca. Leave me alone," he warned.

Becca, the veteran door-banger, walked back to her empty bed. Ulli had told her to think and, for some reason, she had been thinking about God. Not God, really, but Sunday School. Becca had been sent to a progressive Sunday School so she could have a cultural heritage, which consisted mainly of three hundred pounds of green clay someone had donated. Becca spent most of her time making palm trees to stand on sand-decorated shirt cardboards. And she played the role of Rebekah-at-the-well year after year in the annual Genesis pageant. What a natural!

"And Rebekah will be played by," announces Miss Schwartz, rolling her myopic eyes, "RAbecca!"

Ha! Ha! But it is always the young Rebecca she plays, dressed in a striped towel and a lace tablecloth, casting her eyes shyly downward at the servant of Abraham in his father's bathrobe. The good little girl Rebecca, when she longs to play the older and wiser Rebecca, the lady who fooled her husband by disguising one son for another. Oh, how her heart beats to think of that cool calculating Rebecca, cooking up the tender veal in her special sauces, taking skins to sew into a hairy shirt for Jacob to wear. Becca's Golden Illustrated Bible shows that phony Jacob kneeling before his blind old father in a pair of furry gloves, and Rebecca, much younger than Isaac, better preserved, leaning out of the tent on the lookout for poor dumb Esau back from the hunt. What a deception! Maybe her name is a slur, a sin, a birthmark.

Becca walked down the stairs to look for a Bible and more brandy. No Old Testament, only the New, a paperback edition of the New English Bible one of them had purchased for a course long ago. Becca looked for the story of Mary and Martha and fell asleep.

She awakened to the door slamming again. Gerry had left before she could lift her aching head. She found only his morning remains: cornflakes drying on a bowl, instant coffee abandoned. How could he eat? In his study, she found the afghan his mother had knitted for his last birthday, rumpled sheets, the notes for this morning's lecture. Automatically, she began to straighten and pick up.

"Where's Daddy?" Alexy asked, and put her thumb in her mouth as a safeguard.

"He went to work early," Becca whispered, hugging her.

"Dumb Daddy, dopey Daddy," sang Tory, who was working out alliteration that week.

Becca laughed and kissed her. Dumb Daddy, bad Daddy, evil Daddy, crazy Daddy, who wants to separate us, she wanted to shout, but was too well-educated to do that.

Becca dressed them for school in their little doll clothes. Alexy carried a pink plastic pocketbook Becca's mother had sent her. Becca insisted on calling it an attaché case. Tory walked around with a piece of soiled blanket.

She served them breakfast outdoors, something Gerry hated, on their tiny terrace with the neighbor's cats and laundry for guests. It was the one week of the year that every flowering tree was in bloom: cherries and dogwoods holding fast, the heavy lush magnolias opening their pink thighs. This is Paradise, Becca realized in horror and awe.

She had actually been admitted to Paradise and was in grave danger of being expelled from it. Gerry was going to kick her out of Paradise, without a fair trial, and she would never know why.

Is this how Eve felt? wondered Becca, driving through the heavily perfumed streets to her daughters' nursery school. Was it only in the final moment that Eve had looked up and had seen the enormous beauty she must leave? But she had had no chance to think, to ponder the error of her ways, to prepare her defense, to demand a hearing. She ate the apple, and boom! Oh, the wrath of that God, the terror of an Old Testament God, the most male of all males. Fast, swift! Out of the Garden! In Becca's childhood Bible, Eve covered her eyes and her crotch.

"I think you are really in trouble, Becca," said Ulli softly, as Becca sat down in the dining room to cry.

"He was already gone this morning before I woke up."

"Why don't you eat something, Becca? You will feel better."

"I'm not hungry. Uh, I took your advice."

"*Jo?*"

"I drank a whole bottle of brandy."

"I did not say a bottle, Becca."

"You'd better find yourself a lawyer, Becca," John said, grabbing a piece of toast from the silver rack and pulling on a smooth suede jacket.

"A what?"

"A lawyer, an attorney."

"What for?" Oh, God, did she have a headache.

John sat down next to Becca and took her hands, like a child's. "Becca, Gerry says he is going to divorce you. That you have done something terrible."

"I am making you an omelette," Ulli announced from the kitchen.

"I wrote some poems," Becca said miserably. "I think I'm protected by the Bill of Rights or something."

"You have to protect yourself, Becca. I don't think Gerry's talking about poems. He kept muttering about photographs."

"Photographs! Ulli!" Becca whispered.

Ulli stood in the doorway, white eggs poised in her hands, her head wobbling up and down.

Becca watched the eggs open, the yolks slide precariously down the slippery sides of a blue bowl.

Becca knew what it was before she saw the envelope, before she opened it, before she actually looked at the photographs Emmett had taken of her in his living room in Bennington.

She recognized Gerry's expression as familiar, too, that small curve of triumph decorating his lower face. She had seen that expression on her father's face on the Wednesday nights he played cards with his cronies.

Becca stared at Gerry's hand. "Where did you get those?"

"Oh, I've had them for years," Gerry smiled again, involuntarily.

She remembered staring through the opening in the felt cloth that covered the card table, at the lower half of her father's body: slim, polished shoes with perforations, lisle socks with a Jacquard design, tiny garters, like snakes, and up the hairy legs to the mound, the small fruit of her father's center, up to the waist, clinched with the skin of some dead reptile.

Becca had seen that luxurious smile on many male faces, an assortment of car mechanics and repairmen, doctors and professors, surely on Emmett, hidden behind his camera.

"Gerry, give me those!" she shouted.

"Why should I?"

"They're mine!"

"They were sent to me."

"Forget it, never mind. I don't want them. I want them to go away."

"Well, I want them. They'll make terrific evidence in court."

"Evidence for what?"

"I told you, Becca. I intend to divorce you and take the girls with me."

"For what? What have I done wrong?"

"You know goddamned well what I'm talking about. You've been having an affair with Mac."

"Define an affair!"

"Define 'define'!" Gerry chewed on his lips and smirked.

"Oh, shit. We're going to have a Harvard Square conversation. I was never very good at that, Ger, you'd better go find your friend Miriam if you want to talk in circles."

"Is that what it was? Miriam? You've been keeping score, Becca, and you just wanted to even it up? I told you at the time, Becca, that was nothing."

"This is nothing, too." She watched him pass the envelope back and forth between his big hands.

"God, Becca, you must think I'm really stupid. Everybody knows you're having an affair with Mac."

"Who is everybody?"

"Don't play Shylock's daughter with me, Becca."

"Who? I don't know what we're talking about anymore."

"I'm talking about your goddamned affair with Mac."

"I'm not having an affair with Mac. He is my teacher, and I'm very, very fond of him. But, I'm not sleeping with him, if that's how you define an affair."

"His wife seems to think you are."

"His wife said that?" Becca raised an eyebrow. "She knows better than that."

"What the hell does that mean?"

Becca was not sure if Mac's impotency would work in her

favor or against her. "Did you ask Ulli?"

"Oh, Ulli was very busy defending you. She kept babbling about Baskin-Robbins and cooking courses at the Adult School. Liar! I know you tell Ulli everything."

"I don't tell anybody everything. There are pieces of my life no one has ever touched. Those are my secrets, and that's where my poetry comes from."

"Don't give me that crap, Becca. You tell everybody everything. Christ, you spent most of your life on a stage! Why don't you rent a billboard and blow up some of these photographs so everyone can look into your cervix, not just the ladies in your CR group!" He dropped the photos on the floor near her feet.

"How did you get these?" she demanded, grabbing them. "He told me they were . . . gone," she cried.

"I received them the week before we were married!" Gerry shouted and slammed the door in her face.

It was an ordinary manila envelope with a typed label, none of Emmett's classy italic script. The metal clasp came off in her hand as she bent it open; she pulled out the photographs, almost expecting to see herself as a baby or a bride.

There was a heavy pink cast to some of them, blue in others, a few were yellowish, Emmett understood well the veiled aspects of desire his customers demanded. These subtle tones, plus the costumes, gave them an historical look and almost allowed Becca to dismiss the obvious pornographic angles. Emmett had been honest, they were not taken as mementos. Her face was obscured, so she hardly recognized herself. At first, Becca marveled at how pretty and young she looked, the glossy smoothness of her body, the little heart- and crescent-shaped felt moles Emmett had pressed in various places on her breasts and belly. Only slowly did she comprehend the rawness, the exposure, the use.

She stuffed the photographs into the envelope and tiptoed down the hall, downstairs to Gerry. One of her daughters called out in her sleep, not "Mommy!" but "Sheep!" the leftover of today's field trip to a farm. Becca turned around and walked into their room, clutching her envelope, and kneeled by the beds.

Becca's daughters slept in little birch beds stacked up like lifeboats on an ocean liner: two red heads, one with curls, one in short braids. Alexy sucked her thumb vigorously, Tory snored. Becca put her cheek next to Tory's face on her pillow and smelled her closeness: a faint odor of urine, tonight's bubble bath, the staleness of her wet fingers. For a minute, Becca wished to crawl into that bed, to be that little girl, to clutch the Raggedy Ann doll that had been hers.

Mine! she wanted to shout, but it was all hers. These dolls, these little girls, sweet heads and white teeth, like tiny beads on her add-a-pearl necklace, the rows of books someone had read to Becca and Becca now read to them. This was the house that Becca built, this was the life she made.

She wrapped Tory's arms around the doll and went downstairs. Gerry was sitting on the sofa staring into the fireplace. It was warm outside, but he had made a huge blazing fire. Becca remembered he had been an Eagle Scout.

"Oh, Gerry," said Becca sadly, dryly. "Oh, I'm so sorry, so sorry," she hiccupped and began to sob. "Please, please forgive me, let me stay."

"You'd better tell me about those photographs, Rebecca."

"Oh, please don't call me that."

"What? Rebecca?"

"Yes, it sounds so . . . so serious."

"It is serious! You have a lot of trouble understanding that, Becca."

"Okay, I'm sorry. Why did you marry me after you got them?"

"I loved you. I still love you. Besides, you were carrying my child . . . at least, I assume she's my child."

"Oh, yes, she's certainly not Emmett's," Becca said and giggled slightly. "God, what men I pick. I just thought about the men I've been involved with. One's gay, the other impotent, the third one's my grandfather."

"That's very observant of you."

"What?"

"Your 'grandfather,' Becca."

"Oh, Grandpops," she sighed. She went and kneeled at Gerry's feet. "Oh, Gerry, you're the only real thing that's happened to me." She put her arms around his knees and hugged them, crying. "And you married me anyway. Oh, Gerry, please forgive me."

He sat down next to her on the rug and put his arm around her.

"Why did you keep the pictures? Why didn't you destroy them?" she cried.

"I don't know. I thought I might need them someday. And I've been trained to preserve data, not destroy it, Becca, you know that." He took them out and laid them out on the coffee table. "Sometimes late at night I take them out and look at them."

"Gerry!"

"They don't really look like you, Becca."

"I know. They look so beautiful."

"We should have taken more pictures," said Gerry, slyly.

"Oh, God, Gerry! Please destroy them now. Please, let's burn them or something!"

"All right."

"I never really slept with Mac, Gerry. I swear."

"You swear?"

"Cross my heart and hope to die, stick a needle in my eye," said Becca. "I don't give a shit about that course. I'm a terrible poet, Gerry. Really. You can burn the poems, too."

"Becca, are you sure you want me to?" Gerry asked, but less quietly.

Watching them all go up in flames, Becca and Gerry made the best love they ever had.

"Oh Becca, are you really sure?"

"Sure," asked Becca incredulously. "You are all I have ever wanted."

"Ah!" Ulli breathed in horror. She did not recognize Becca for a full minute. "Why, Becca?"

"What does it make you think of, Ulli? Auschwitz? The good sisters of the *Sacre Cœur*? Joan of Arc, Jo March? Oh, you never read *Little Women*," Becca babbled. "Gertrude Stein? Come on, let's play charades. Two words, Ulli. It's a place."

"Becca . . . *so* short?" Ulli was saying.

Becca had meant to make a statement about her antecedents in the shetel: the ceremony of cutting the bride's hair, or shaving it, Becca had never been sure. How had it been done? Was there a special person and a party afterwards? Judaism was a strange religion, given to moments of strange celebration. If you gave a party for prick-trimming, why not a haircut, too? Maybe a ladies' luncheon, the predecessor of the bridal shower?

Over the years, Becca had formed a picture of the bride, sitting on a high kitchen stool. While the men were out drinking or praying or something, her sisters danced in a circle around her, some laughing, some crying, while her mother took the kitchen shears and . . . snip, snip.

Becca was never able to find out the answers. Ancient customs were a subject as loaded as sex or cancer in her house, and no one answered with more than a shrug or a slap or a finger shaking against sealed lips. Rebecca, lying on the heavy linen pillowslips of her grandparents' double bed for an afternoon nap, became very good at recognizing who's who, the little old ladies with the thatched-roof wigs jabbering in the courtyard.

Whatever, Becca had finally figured out that this had something to do with men, with God who was male, with a woman belonging to her husband, with the sin of being born a woman, with the sudden and permanent end to childhood.

"It was your shining glory," Ulli said, reciting a shampoo commercial she had made in the late fifties.

Becca had cut off her hair, those waves and billows, and now she took a grocery bag and emptied it into Ulli's lap.

"Here," she said, before she burst into tears, "I thought maybe you could make a pillow out of it, or something."

PART III

One

Some years later, Becca sits on the w.c. in a row house in the
Islington section of London. Somewhere in the night, the
wife of the British professor who owns this house is sitting
on Becca's toilet in New Jersey. Such are the advantages of
an academic life.

For her birthday, they have gone to a famous restaurant,
which they can barely afford, for dinner. The cream and
butter seemed to have formed a permanent alliance in
Becca's stomach. Meanwhile, Gerry, who has been acting
like a small boat in a choppy sea, jumps out of bed, retches,
and vomits between the bedroom and the bathroom sink.

"Uh, sorry," he groans, looking up at Becca's legs.

"Gerry, are you all right?"

"Oh, Becca, I . . ." he says and vomits again. "I feel so . . ."

"Take it easy. It's okay, Gerry. Really. It was the fucking cream. Clotted cream, whew, what a name!" Becca throws on a robe and runs to the kitchen for paper towels. "Here, darling, take a nice bath and I'll clean up." She stoops gracefully and starts to run the tub.

"Oh, Becca," he says.

She sees there are tears in his eyes, which she attributes to the vomiting, but they start to flow down his face. Becca helps Gerry into the tub. The water is just lukewarm; the water heater in this house is the size of a thermos bottle. "I'll boil some water. Are you okay?"

"Oh, Becca," he sniffles. He is really weeping now, large tears plopping into the water like raindrops into a puddle.

Becca is truly alarmed. "Shall I call a doctor, Gerry?"

"No, no," he says, but doesn't stop crying.

Becca pours in some boiling water, carefully, near the back of the tub and settles on the edge, soaping his back and neck. "Feel better?" she asks.

"Oh, Becca, Becca," Gerry sobs, "you're so good to me. . . ."

Becca hopes he will stop crying soon or the water will be cold. She is trying to remember when she has seen Gerry cry before. He claims to have cried several times, all of them political assassinations, she is sure.

"Oh, Becca," he is saying, "I've been so bad . . . so bad. . . ."

"Huh?" The soap circles she is creating have become bigger and bigger and have slowed down.

"I've . . . oh, Becca," he grabs her hand. "I've been having a little affair."

"Ug?" Becca makes a small belch. The soap catapults out of her hand and lands in the clothes hamper. What is a little affair vs. a big affair? she wonders already.

"With Angel."

"With Angel?" His research assistant.

"Yes," he sniffles. "May I have my glasses, Becca? I'd like to organize my thoughts."

"Organize your thoughts?" marvels Becca. Is he going to lecture?

Gerry starts to laugh a little with relief, but stops when he sees Becca's face. He comes clean in the bathtub: Two years . . . the meetings in San Francisco . . . pushed together all day long . . . Angel rather attractive, don't you think? "Not like you, of course. . . ."

"No, younger," says Becca, who discerned the difference immediately.

"Then, there were the meetings in the Caribbean, and a trip out to the Coast in September, Boston in the spring, sometimes in the office. . . ." lists Gerry, warming to his subject.

"Under the desk, I suppose."

"No, no, on that old sofa. The one we used to have in front of the fireplace in our old apartment."

"Shmuck!" Becca shouts.

"Oh, Becca, darling, it doesn't mean . . ."

"Just another celebratory fuck?"

"What?"

"Miriam. Under the desk in your carrel. Remember?"

"Celebratory fuck? Did I say that?" Gerry smiles. "Becca, you make me wince."

"Well, you make me puke!" screams Becca.

"What about Mac?"

"Oh, God. Are we keeping score again? Isn't that what you said a few years ago?"

"Becca, do you remember everything I said?"

Becca remembers a lot of things. "What are you planning to do about it?"

"I don't know." His color is returning and he is splashing off the soap. "What do you think I should do?" Gerry asks seriously as he pulls the drain.

"I think you should get the hell out of here."

"But we're going to France with the girls tomorrow," he objects. "Hand me a towel, Becca, I'm getting cold."

Becca throws him a damp facecloth and slams the door. She should have poured boiling water over his genitals while she had the chance.

"Aren't we going to France tomorrow?" he asks, suddenly behind her in the bedroom.

"Don't say 'we,' white man, and get your hands off me. I think you should take this opportunity to go home and screw Angelica some more."

"Oh, Becca, what will you tell the girls?"

"The truth."

"What's that?"

"That their father would rather screw Angelica than live with their mother."

"Oh, Becca, I didn't think you were going to be like this at all."

"Oh, I'm so sorry. Excuse me." Where has Becca read that the dream of every middle-class man is to have his wife and mistress living under one roof? "Did you think we were going to all live happily ever after? Well, think again, shmuck!"

Gerry spins Becca around by the shoulders and shouts at her, "Okay, Becca, okay, you bitch. You want the truth. Here is the truth. Angelica loves me and I love her. She's fresh and sweet and young. And she loves me and I love her. There, bitch! Aw shit," Gerry sighs, "what can I say? It feels so good."

Becca closes her eyes. She imagines Angelica's dirty feet, her long toes almost touching as she clasps them around Gerry's spreading middle. The tips of her knees stand up curved and shiny. Becca has watched her stride into a room a dozen times, her long legs in the tightest jeans. She has watched her take a napkin in her long fingers and tear it into a strip of lace. Or wrap her own long, blond hair slowly around her wrist.

Once, Becca had taken Tory and Alexy out to the farm where Angel lived with some other graduate students so they could ride the horses. Becca had stood with the girls watching Angel, her colorless eyes blazing with fury and determination, as she jumped fences made of overturned oil cans and ceiling beams.

"That's what I'm going to do," Tory had informed Becca and pulled her hand loose.

Becca has really missed the boat, the last generation of women to beg and cook. She imagines herself as the Colossus of Rhodes, straddling both sides of the harbor in second position.

"The trouble with wives these days is they don't die in childbirth," Becca says softly. "Gerry, hey, Ger," says Becca, tapping him on the back. The bastard is sound asleep.

"Ha? Wha?" He rolls over and looks at Becca, his features disassembled from sleep and vomiting. "What do you want, Becca? I'll clear out in the morning, I promise."

She snaps on the light, moves it so it shines on his face, a little something she picked up from the movies. "I want the years back," she tells Gerry.

"Come on, Becca."

"The years you owe me. Isn't that what you're trying to do? Well, I'd like the years back, also, the years . . . all those years and years, the years," says Becca, over and over, hugging herself, rocking back and forth.

"Go to sleep," says Gerry, reaching over her bent body to turn off the light. "You'll survive."

"Well, aren't you glad we came to France, anyway?" says Becca brightly. Rain hangs off the roof of their hotel like sheets of black crepe.

The children ignore her. This is Becca's odyssey, not theirs. They drop strawberry jam, thick as rubies, on their nightgowns, on their fat dirty toes, on the heavily starched sheets, missing the croissants completely. Becca tries to smile all the time; American children, they are unused to these small white chambers. Where is the color TV? Where is the ice machine? Where is the BATHROOM? they shouted after their initial inspection tour last night.

"There is the bathroom." Becca explains, pointing: "Washbasin, shower . . ."

"What's that?"

"The bidet. It's for cleaning your bottom."

"Where's the toilet? It's the only thing I use," Alexy whines.

"I'll use the tushy sink," says Tory, before Becca can stop her.

Unable to sleep at night, Becca sits in the dimly lit bathroom, on the floor, reading. Every afternoon on the way back from the beach, she buys herself another small bottle of cognac and a new paperback from the small assortment of Penguins at the local *tabac*. For some reason, behind the Maigrets and James Bonds, there is a selection of D. H. Lawrence. Mainly his travel books: Mexico. Becca remembers her discovery of Lawrence one warm sophomore month. All those burning loins. Becca had begun to think of loins as cuts of meat, pork or lamb.

During the war, Becca's mother insists, while other people were eating macaroni, they had lamb chops every night. Where did all those lamb chops come from? Those lamb chop coupons? Becca liked to imagine her spotless mother and the butcher: prints in the sawdust, the ripe odor of blood, the rack of bent cardboard numbers tumbled . . . all for a chop.

Women have been trading favors for lamb chops for

centuries. Look at Angelica and her thesis. Where was Becca the day she arrived at the door with her suitcase and portable hair dryer?

Becca was changing the linens in the guest room, putting on the flowered sheets that sat in the closet with unwrapped cakes of French soap beneath them. Becca was baking an apple pie for their dinner and carrying real iced tea to the garden where Gerry and Angel were outlining her duties for the fall semester.

"Just for a few days," Gerry said, when Angel burned a hole in Becca's teapot, giving herself a facial.

"She's an *orphan*, Becca, no family," said Gerry, when Angel arrived for breakfast, Becca's blue sweater draped around her shoulders like a cloak.

"Hey, Becca," said Angel the first night. "I forgot a toothbrush. Is yours the red one?"

In the morning, there are suddenly dozens of little foil jelly packages on the breakfast tray. The waiter sets it on the table, which Becca tries to clear of magic markers and coloring books, one hand keeping her robe closed.

"You like the music?" the waiter asks, indicating the wealth of jelly with fluttering eyelashes. He catches a glimpse of himself in the mirror, pulls up his collar, slicks down his hair. "And the dance?"

Becca, unprepared for an early morning poll, takes a step away from him.

Luckily, he answers for her. "*Certainement*. All the American ladies like the music and the dancing."

Tory and Alexy watch carefully from their side of the room.

"Tonight I will come for you. We will dance. *Oui?*"

"Oh, *non*. *Non*," says Becca, shaking her head, backing against the table. "*Les enfants* . . ."

"*Non*, the hotel will watch the children." He flashes his

teeth at her.

He must be at least sixteen, Becca realizes. "Impossible!" she says firmly, closing the door after him.

The next morning a different waiter brings the tray. They are back to one jelly apiece. The girls, catching on right away, glare at her.

"Well, what shall we do today?" she asks brightly, flipping through the Michelin, *vert.*

"I was saving them for Daddy," Tory shouts, pulling the last jelly out of Becca's hand.

"Do you suppose we'll ever see him again?" Alexy sighs, dramatically.

"Of course. Don't spill chocolate on the sheets." Why is Becca so sure of this?

"Why are you so sure?" asks Tory. "He's left you."

Is that an expression or is she merely using words accurately for a change? "Well, he hasn't left you. He'll always be your father." Sure, there will always be an England, too, thinks Becca through a big hole in her heart.

"But where will we live when we get home?"

Becca, who has been asking herself that all week, tries to answer positively. "The Talbotts will be out of the house in a few weeks and we'll go home and see Christoph and Ulli and you'll go back to your school. . . ."

"Will you have the big bedroom or will Daddy and Angel?" Tory asks.

"That isn't the way it's done, dummy," Alexy says. "The Daddy moves out and the Mommy gets the house. Usually." She thinks for a while. "Sometimes, like Tommy's Daddy stayed, but his Mommy ran off with someone. . . . Anyway, the person who gets the children, gets the house."

Whew, thinks Becca, where does she get her information? "Don't worry, darling, you and Muffie can move into the big bedroom when we get home." Muffie is Tory's cat.

"She's lying," Alexy tells her sister. "The minute we get

home, she'll forget."

"She will not."

"She will."

"Could we refer to her as something besides 'she'?" Becca asks.

"Rebecca always forgets," Alexy says with final dignity.

Little bitches, thinks Becca, wiping butter from the blankets. If she didn't feel so guilty, she'd beat them with a hanger.

Two

Standing on the beach at Arromanches, Becca lights a cigarette and looks out to sea. It is pouring again. Everyone is inside at the War Museum, viewing dioramas of battles, faceless mannequins in different uniforms, a BBC documentary on building the bridge. Becca watches an old man spit on her car; it has German license plates. She wants to go over to him and explain the ways of Volkswagen International to him. She wishes to replace the big D with a yellow star. She needs to grab him and reassure him. "Members of my family tapdanced through Auschwitz," she'll say. But it strikes her as being pretentious; she has used the line too often.

Becca remembers the photographs in yellowing *Life*

magazines piled in the basement, photos of American boys running up these beaches. This had been her father's war, too. Her father, that skinny stranger, smelling of cigarettes and hair-oil, invader of their soprano household. The first act he performed after returning from the war was to move Becca's crib out of her mother's pink bedroom. He says Becca screamed and scratched and bit him. No wonder she needed a shrink, with such tidy Freudian acts performed in early childhood.

From the pocket of her raincoat, Becca withdraws a much folded letter, forwarded from London. A few melting Smarties are stuck to one side, and she pops them into her mouth as she reads Ulli's letter again. It is very difficult to read, seems to have been written in the dark on a moving train. Ink is missing in several places. Becca has to give it the kind of attention she used to give the decoding of Dick Tracy's secret messages at breakfast.

Dearest Becca:
Excuse please the delay and my hand. . . . I am so glad Sister Marguerite will not see it. I hope it has stopped raining. _____ hand shaking and forgetting some words it seems. They think _____arthritis maybe, but finally I will go to see Dr. Ross for a scan of my brain. . . .

Guy Ross! Becca thinks with alarm. He is the husband of Ulli's doubles partner. Becca is certain he does surgery with a tennis racquet.

So. They will have to explore the region, they say. I will know by _____.

There is something about summer plans: Christopher's camp, Becca's tenants; and then, John's handwriting, startlingly large and firm, at the bottom of the page.

*They removed a large tumor from Ulli's brain July 10. There is no
reason to come home before planned. I think it may alarm Ulli. They
are making more tests and she is still in the hospital. Hope for the
best. xxxxxs and ooooooos. John.*

Xxxxxxs and ooooos, thinks Becca. Grandma Rosie
signed all her correspondence with those, too. Becca feels as
if she stepped off the top of an escalator when she reads this
letter. There is nothing else, no further news from
America's favorite anchorman. But Becca is afraid to call,
frightened to tackle the French telephone system, maybe
really afraid of the truth. It is better to live with the
unknown. So she selects a color postcard of the American
cemetery at Omaha Beach from the Museum Shop and
vows to write Ulli.

In the car, the children are hungry. Alexy, who couldn't be
bribed, begged, threatened to eat, who spent five minutes
on one breast and left the other hanging like a ripe
eggplant, eats all the time. The backseat resembles a Pop
Art collage: empty Kit-Kat wrappers, dusty crepes, moldy
sausages, sticky empty bottles of orange Fanta.
    "I'm hungry!"
    "I'm starving!"
Becca glances madly around the ancient stone streets of
Bayeux for a pair of golden arches. Finally, she spots a
snack bar with plasticized photos of *croque monsieurs* and
saucissons in bleeding pastels. *"Là!"* she points. *"C'est une*
McDonalds *à la française!"*
    "Oh, Mummy." There is audible sighing and squirming.
Her French embarrasses her daughters as much as their
newly acquired British accents bother Becca.
    She maneuvers her car into a spot Gerry would have
found illegal and *dangereux* and slams the door in defiance.
Sometimes, Becca feels courage swelling like Popeye's mus-

cles do when he eats spinach.

In the restaurant, on warm dry planks covered with checkered oilcloths, they are forced to share the table with a tall blond man, dressed in a huge yellow slicker.

"Don't speak English," Tory whispers to her sister, as if there is an alternative. "Then he won't talk to us."

"All right, Alex, Tory, what do you want? There . . ."

"I can read," Alexy says coldly.

"*Pardon,*" Becca replies and tries to dry out her long hair with her fingers. "Well, what do you want?"

"Chips and Cokes, mostly." Tory is chewing on her thumb until it bleeds. Becca pulls it out of her mouth.

"*Trois saucissons, deux pommes frites pour les enfants. Et deux Cocoa, et un Calvados . . . grand.*" Becca indicates with a wide spread of her fingers.

One daughter looks at the ceiling, the other selects the floor. Becca stares at the laughing cow poster over the *caisse.*

"Well, she says finally, when the food comes, "after lunch we'll go see the Bayeux Tapestry . . ."

"What?"

"Don't talk with your mouth full, please. A tapestry is like a big sampler. You know, like needlepoint, the pillows Grandma Judy makes."

"Embroidery," says Alexy. "Bo-ring." Tory just stuffs her mouth with *frites.*

"Americans?" the blond man asks suddenly, pleasantly.

Becca looks at him. He is so fair he appears almost transparent, the Invisible Man Tory received for her birthday last year.

"She is," says Tory. "We're English, you know."

Becca smiles at him apologetically and sighs. His hands are folded neatly on the edge of the table, as in a prayer. He has long fingers with wide flat nails like spoons. Becca wonders if he is a pianist. "I . . ."

"Please," he says. "I do not mean to interrupt the lecture.

Continue."

"Well, it was done by the wife of William the Conqueror to commemorate his victory over the English in . . ."

"The Battle of Hastings, 1066. Boy, do you think we're dumb," says Alexy. "Can I have another Coke?"

"I will get it," says the blond man, quickly. "And may I refill yours?"

"Our mother drinks like a fish," says Tory, companionably.

"Excuse me," says Becca, "I left my guidebook in the car."

When she returns, the girls have draped themselves over each side of their mystery guest.

"Remember what we told you about . . ." Tory puts her finger to her lips.

"This is Dr. Silversword," Alexy says.

"Dr. Silversword?" Becca can barely refrain from peeking down at his jeans.

"Sven. I tell them Silversword. It is the translation, but easier for children, I think."

"Is Mrs. Silversword here?"

"*Nej,* in Stockholm. Is not a holiday if both go."

Becca chokes on her Calvados.

Sven reaches over efficiently and grabs her around the upper chest. "I am doctor in Sweden," he explains.

"An internist?"

"I am a breast specialist," he says. "But I am, as you Americans say, an 'ass man' myself."

Becca swallows so she will not choke again. "My . . . my best friend is Swedish," she says stupidly.

"*Jo?*"

"Ulli. What is her last name? I can't remember. Ulli . . ."

"Sweden is a very small country, I think, but not that small," he smiles.

"I'm sorry. You don't happen to know anything about brain tumors, do you?"

"Not so much, but if you are worried . . ." he says, sympathetically.

Becca pulls Ulli's letter out of her pocket. Wet, it is even less legible than before. How ridiculous, clutching to the first kind stranger she meets. "Never mind," she says, putting it back.

"Do you stay around here?" he asks.

"We're down the coast in a ghastly hotel. It's okay for me, really, but it isn't much fun for the girls."

"Ah, then you must change to where I am staying. It is very near, with a swimming pool and close to the beach. I think that is important, do you?" he asks the girls.

"I don't know," says Becca.

"Oh, please, Mummy!"

"Pretty please!"

"Do you think there's room?"

"I will call if you like," he says.

"All right," she agrees.

"Can we go now!" Tory jumps up.

"First," says Sven, "we must see the Bayeaux tapestry. Then we will swim. *Jo?*"

The girls follow him to the telephone.

What do men do, what powers do they possess, that even small children recognize their authority immediately? wonders Becca, watching him.

Sven is seated at a small table on the terrace when Becca comes down for dinner.

"Do you mind if we talk about brain tumors for a minute?" she asks.

"*Jo*, it is okay." But he wrinkles his forehead.

Becca fishes out Ulli's letter, which is becoming a part of every outfit, from the pocket of her dress and hands it to Sven.

He reads it carefully, turning the pages over and over,

looking for missing clues. "It does not say much."

"Tell me about brain tumors," insists Becca.

"I do not know you so well, Becca. Are you sure?"

"Sure," says Becca. "I am sure." She wants to put her head down on his lap. This afternoon, standing in the cold sea for several hours, he taught both her daughters how to water-ski.

"Ah," he breathes. "If it is malignant, and the letter suggests it is so, it can be . . . if you are lucky and it is in one place and operable and there is treatment, maybe, it can be arrested for a while."

"How long?"

"A year, maybe two . . ."

"A year? Maybe two?" Becca stares at him.

He takes her hand. "That is if you are lucky, Becca. If it is a kind that is not operable, then it sits inside the head like a spider's web." He stretches out his fingers over her head. "And it is all over the brain. You cannot really touch it all. Then, we talk about . . . months."

"No!" says Becca, pulling away from him. "No!"

"Becca, Becca," he says, grabbing onto her shoulders. "This was not a good idea. I should not have said this to you. I do not know in Ulli's case . . ."

"But she's going to die?"

"Ah, Becca, we are all dying. None of us is immortal. Surely, you must know that." He looks at his hands. "She is a good friend?"

"The best," says Becca. She sees her daughters running around the edge of the dining room, stealing rolls from empty tables. "What did my daughters tell you about me?"

"Ah, they are very charming. Your daughters."

"Ha!" snorts Becca.

"They do not say too much. They tell me your husband has just left and you are alone." He takes hold of her hand again.

"Are you sure you want to hear this?"

"*Jo,* I want to hear it all," he says patting the hand.

"I'm not sure why I'm telling you any of this. . . ."

"I am used to it. You know, in Sweden, we try not to look like doctors. We do not wear white smocks or anything, but still people always know who we are."

"Well," says Becca, taking a big gulp of wine. "I was the perfect little girl . . . who was to guess I wouldn't grow up to be the perfect woman?"

"So," he says, "that is the source of the problem. You are too perfect."

"I shall reveal my imperfections shortly," Becca promises. He laughs. "Would you like to dance?"

"It won't be on the dance floor," she says, taking his hand. They move close to the band; Becca hums between her teeth.

"Ah, that is true. You dance very well."

"I was a dancer . . . I wanted to be a dancer. In my youth."

"Your youth, Becca? What is this?"

"This is probably a repressed, latent adolescence." Becca looks over to their table, where her daughters sit, like a pair of miniature *doyennes.* They're pimping for me, thinks Becca briefly. Actually, they've done all right.

"You are a very beautiful woman, Becca," says Sven.

"I'm a very needy woman," she corrects. "My needs are flashing all over me like a traffic signal." She places her hand on the back of his neck. "This is very romantic," she says, pointing to the moon and the stars.

"It is supposed to be," says Sven, moving closer.

"I didn't know you Swedes were so romantic."

"I have some Norwegian blood," he admits.

"Norwegians!" laughs Becca. "I can't imagine . . . God, I keep getting pictures of trolls in my head."

"Ah, Becca, you do not know of Munch? Of Ibsen? There is a black streak that runs through every soul! Why do people think it is sun and guitars and vineyards that produce passion? Passion, Becca," Sven announces, "passion is black, not red. It is deep down," Sven says anatomically. "With the pain."

In his room, the children sent off with money for the pinball machines, the *ne pas déranger* sign swinging precariously from the doorknob, Becca wanders through foreign terrain without a guidebook, only a prayer. She stares at this stranger in alarm: she has never even seen an uncircumcised penis before. She misses Gerry, his predictable comings and goings and patterns and tunes. She will have to improvise. This is worse than losing your virginity, she decides. There, at least, the mantle of love protected you.

Becca and Sven, spread on the sheets, two X's of arms and legs. They are both pale and gold, there are threads of gold and red everywhere as in a lavish medieval panel; they seem to be covered in an aureole of their own light. She runs her hands over him, and suddenly, there is the familiarity: the sharp bones at two sides of the hips, the blond, almost straight, silky pubic hair, the pale pink of his nipples. It is Ulli, she is thinking of, of course. Ulli, the golden girl, silk soft, pale pink Ulli. This man is Ulli, with a magic rod.

With Sven, Becca realizes that Ulli has been her great love, her *grande passion,* the romantic gesture she has searched her life for. That was it. Being women, their love has never been put to this test, it has grown with honesty, like the love for children, without lust.

Petal pure, thinks Becca, as this strange man enters her silently, and she moans, cries out without warning, "Ulli!"

Three

John is in front of customs, interviewing Andre Previn for
the six o'clock news. Becca sees him through the smudged
windows of the customshouse, sees Christopher, taller, his
hair bleached almost white from the summer sun, carrying
John's attaché case, and starts waving wildly. "Oh, John!"
she cries, "Christopher!" and rushes to give them both
kisses. Christopher pulls away slightly, rubs her kiss away
with the back of his hand.

"Where's Ulli?" Becca asks.

John turns around as if struck. "She's home resting,
Becca. Oh, God, don't you understand what's been going on
around here?" He takes her elbow and starts toward the
parking lot, microphones and wires dangling, cameras still

whirling behind him. The girls follow with Christopher, arms linked, singing "The Star Spangled Banner."

"No, I don't understand what's going on here," Becca objects, trying to keep up with John's pace. "Oh, please make them all stop."

John waves his arm and the cameras disappear magically; John and Becca are just two people standing on the curb with a lot of luggage.

"I'll bring the car," John says and exits quickly.

"Mommy, can I give Christopher the . . . ?" Alexy whispers, spitting, in her ear.

"Oh shit, I don't care," Becca snaps. She has purchased an elegant unpackable straw hat for Ulli and it is pinching her head. She takes it off and rubs her temples.

"You don't have to be so bitchy," Tory says.

John piles the suitcases into the trunk and hands Becca the keys. It is a new car, an enormous Mercedes, dark, the color of a bruised plum, gloomy as a tomb. "Becca," he begins slowly, selecting his words carefully; no one has provided him with a script for this. "Ulli's been sick."

"I know that," Becca says. "She's home, isn't she? I can see her, can't I?"

"Yes, yes, of course. She wants you to come for dinner tonight. I told her your plane wouldn't be in until late so she would take her nap." It is an awful confession for him to make. He looks at his nails, pink and highly buffed. "She's changed, Becca."

"I'm a big girl, John. I'll behave."

"That isn't what I'm trying to tell you, Becca." He peruses his shoe tassels.

"I'm sorry. I'm tired and everything is so, so . . . ah, unusual. What do you want, Alexy?" Alexy is pulling on her arm and whispering in her ear again. Becca shakes her head. "Can Christopher come to play and I'll bring him home when we come for dinner?" Becca asks.

"He'd like that, Becca. He really missed you all. We all did."

"Oh, John," says Becca, giving him another hug. "I'll take care of everything."

"Becca," John says, closing the car door for her. "You'd better keep the car. I think Gerry took yours."

"Om," says Becca. Gerry. And Ulli. Missing in action.

"Just drive on the right side," says Alexy, settling into the plush back seat with a Tintin.

Becca drives down the familiar and ugly highway. She composes a grocery list; she wants to eat corn, hamburgers and strawberry shortcake. She wants to bite off and chew America as fast as she can. She has come home. She wishes to be protected by every plastic artifact of American life. She didn't know she felt this way; she lets the children drink Cokes and eat Twinkies in the car.

At home: no Gerry. There are gaps like missing teeth in the bookshelves, closets are empty; no car, no Muffie.

"I don't know where the hell Muffie is!" Becca shouts at Tory, who is crying.

"Well, maybe Daddy knows," sniffles Tory.

"Maybe," agrees Becca, but where is Daddy? No phone number is hanging neatly on the babysitter's emergency clipboard.

Becca does loads of wash in her big white machines. She fills the hibachi with charcoal and wipes off the terrace furniture. Her geraniums have all died and been replaced with the wrong ones, pink ones. They remind Becca of Sven's skin.

"Well, what's new with you, Christopher?" asks Becca, loading the dishwasher.

"My mother's dying," he tells her, selecting an ice cream from the freezer.

"Oh, Christoph, she's not dying." Is she? "She's been very sick, but she's getting better every day."

"Nope. She's dying. I heard Daddy tell the maid last week," he says and deposits the wrapper in Becca's open hand.

They watch John on the six o'clock news. He is wearing different clothes, he looks tanned and relaxed and happy. He jokes with the sports announcer about the Mets' chances. They watch him, their mouths full of America.

Madison Avenue has discovered foot odor in Becca's absence; three commercials, one after another, warn her of the dire results of this offense. Actually, Becca notices a sharp odor in the playroom, the children are beginning to stink. Becca remembers, oh, how wonderful their little bald heads smelled, a combination of milk and powder. Decay is starting to set in, they are growing old. Alexy is sprouting mounds of breasts. What is she going to do with them? Becca wonders.

The children stare, hypnotized by the light of the TV screen. Becca looks at them. She has passed through life, like a good crossing guard, looking to the left and to the right, for imminent disaster, but not really believing in the possibility of it. Now it is here.

A long table has been set in the arbor, everywhere white candles flicker against the dusk. Platters of pink and gray herrings alternate with bowls of steaming potatoes and sour cream. There is a stack of round crisp bread and a tiny wooden tub holds softened sweet butter. A frozen bottle of acquavit leans from a silver bucket. The Last Supper, Becca thinks, involuntarily, and forces herself to look at Ulli.

Ulli sits at the head of the table, a clothespin doll with pipe-cleaner limbs. Ulli's right arm dangles lifelessly by her side, her watch strapped to the wrist, like a child's from the dime store.

"Ulli!" Becca breathes sharply and catches sight of the scarf tied to her head. Where is Ulli's hair? . . . her cornsilk hair, hair the color of a yellow Crayola? Becca pulls off the straw hat she had bought for Ulli and hides it under some bushes.

"Becca, you do not mind if I do not get up. . . ."

"Oh, Ulli," Becca cries and runs across the terrace to embrace her. Nothing, she thinks, I am holding nothing. Ulli's breasts flatten against hers, bone knobs stick from her back, her shoulders, neck.

"Ah, Becca, is it so bad?" Ulli asks, tenderly, taking hold of Becca's hand. "I have grown used to me, I suppose."

"No, no," Becca gulps, "it's very *raffiné*, Ulli."

"*Raffiné*, like Auschwitz, Becca."

"Hey Ulli," Becca smiles, recovering slightly. "That's my line. I make the jokes around here, remember? Don't turn funny on me, please."

"Ah, Becca, I am so glad you are home. I have wanted to tell someone so many things, but they . . . John cannot listen to it. He can deal with bad things only if they are on the television. And Christopher . . ."

"Ulli, I'm home. I won't leave you again."

"Do you know? When they shaved my head for the surgery," Ulli says, laughing a little, "I think of you. Do you remember when we took that course in photography in . . . Ah, when was it? My memory is not so good."

"Before Tory was born."

"*Jo*, you were pregnant. There was so little room, I remember, in that booth, to move around. Well, and you asked me if the nuns shaved their heads."

"Yes, I remember," Becca says quietly. Have they become a memory already?

"And you told me about your nightmares about the old women?"

"With the thatched-hut wigs."

"*Jo*," Ulli laughs. "And when you cut off your hair . . . Ah, Becca, it was so short."

"My last romantic gesture," sighs Becca, avoiding looking at Ulli's head again. "Have you seen Gerry?"

"I have been busy," says Ulli. "John had lunch with him last week, I think."

"I didn't know they were such good friends," Becca smirks.

"He needs someone to talk to, too."

"He has someone. Angelica of the blonder pastures."

"John says it is midlife crisis."

Becca laughs. "Good old trendy Gerry. He always has to be the first on the block to wear the latest sociological label."

"Do you think it has something to do with Mac?"

"I paid for that!" Becca says. "It's not Mac . . . shall I make a list? Emmett and Selma and Miriam under the desk and coming of age on Long Island . . . oh, shit, what am I going to do?" She starts crying, although she didn't want to.

"I do not know, Becca," says Ulli sadly. "Perhaps, you can write poetry. I would like to be able to think of you writing poetry."

Ulli has always had a shaky sense of English tenses, but Becca is listening carefully now for clues of immortality. "Oh, Ulli, I'm not a poet, I'm not a dancer . . . I'm a lousy housewife and I just lost the second half of that word. I don't know what I'm going to do or what rights I have or if I have any money. I guess I'll have to call my father. At least he can give me some legal advice."

"Eat something, Becca." Ulli pushes the bowls towards her. "This is *matjes* herring and that is *inlagd sill* . . ."

Becca's voice cracks, she puts down her fork. She cannot eat. "Of course, my parents will think it's all my fault. That I didn't change my underwear or wash my floors frequently enough."

"You are not to blame, Becca. There is no one to blame in these situations. Look at me," says Ulli, using her one good hand to make a presentation of herself. "Who would you blame for this?"

"Oh, that's easy," says Becca, jumping up. "I blame God! Asleep on the job or making a mistake on His wish list for the year!"

"What?"

"Ulli, there is this very serious holiday called Yom Kippur, the Day of Atonement. It is very, very serious; you're supposed to fast. Can you imagine a Jewish holiday without food? When I was a little girl, I would go to the shul with my grandmother and sit with the women. God, you could have suffocated from the Arpège. It was like walking into Bonwit's. Anyway, what God does on Yom Kippur is sit in Heaven and decide who is going to perish and how. Oh, the prayer book went into wonderful detail: plague, fire; in the fifties they probably inserted atomic disaster. And I would look around wondering who wouldn't be here next year. . . ." Becca stops abruptly, Ulli is crying. "Oh, Ulli, I'm sorry, I'm not being funny. . . ." Becca puts her arms around her.

"It is all right, Becca. I am just tired. I think God lost interest in this sinner years ago."

"When He left you upstairs in bed with Uncle Lars."

"Ah, Becca, you remember."

"Of course, I remember. Who could forget a story like that?"

"And our visit at the Cape?"

"Of course, Ulli, I remember everything."

"Ah, good. Someone will remember and it will not all be gone. There is so little. . . ."

"Look, Ulli, this past-tense stuff is ridiculous. I'm here. You're going to get better."

"So this time I get to be Lazarus in the story," Ulli says, tiredly.

"Absolutely," agrees Becca. "As soon as I get my Christ act together."

Four

"Well, I feel about as private as Hester Prynne these days," Becca tells Ulli.

"Ah, Becca, you and your heroines," sighs Ulli. It is early fall, but she is dressed in a heavy coat and muffler and gloves.

News of Gerry's departure has reached the town, eliciting swift response. The doctors call first, as if they have some prior claim to Becca's body. The children's pediatrician offers to make house calls for pending vaccinations. Husbands of friends, neighbors, the gym teacher at the girls' school, all offer to fix things. Although Becca knows the damage is rampant, they are sure they have already located the source of the problem. Sight unseen.

Becca is not interested. She is busy reversing scientific inevitability for Ulli, taking care of Christopher, being flippant to absent Gerry and vulnerable for her fickle daughters. Three times a week, she drives Ulli to the hospital for radiation treatments.

In the car, sitting down, it is easy to pretend they are on their way to the grocery store or a movie. But when they arrive at the outpatient entrance to the hospital, there is a sharp, swift detailed dose of reality. Becca hops quickly out of the car, rushing to the other side to open the door and catch Ulli as she tumbles out. Ulli's useless right hand hangs by her side, Becca moves behind her lopsided shuffling gait. Ulli's head falls to rest on Becca's shoulder, so that for the first time, Becca is taller.

"Becca, why will you not get me a wheelchair? It will be easier for you."

"No. You don't need a wheelchair, Ulli." Becca makes her daily vow not to cry in front of Ulli, opens a door with her hip, remembers Ulli lifting heavy bricks to build a barbecue one summer. Ulli, bending in a plié, her smooth tanned arms curved, her slim manicured hands supporting the bricks.

"Becca, go. Go shop or something. It will take a long time," Ulli says, as the nurse comes for her. "Do not forget to eat lunch today. . . ."

But Becca sits like a penitent in the waiting room, the survivor's room, she calls it, listening to atrocities traded with the casualness of recipes or knitting patterns.

"Well, they had to scrape off a layer of skin for that test. . . ."

". . . and they removed most of the lung last year. . . ."

"All she had left was a hole in the middle of her face. I couldn't even look at her."

Becca sits politely with a notebook she is supposed to be filling with questions for her lawyer, making elaborate grocery lists. She is becoming a gourmet cook; it is easy in Ulli's kitchen, with annotated recipes and well-seasoned pans. Putting on Ulli's apron is like Dorothy stepping into the magic red slippers.

" 'Follow the yellow brick road, follow the yellow brick road,' " sings Becca and does a quick shuffle, shuffle, step, step, for Ulli, wrapped in a blanket in the rocking chair in the corner.

"That is almost right, Becca," Ulli says, sampling a tomato sauce. "I think it is time to ask Gerry to dinner."

"Ho, ho, Ulli," laughs Becca, rolling her eyes, imagining a Norman Rockwell Thanksgiving scene, but with everyone in blue jeans. "The way to a man's heart is through his stomach."

"*Jo,* Becca."

"Let me clue you, Ulli, the way to a man's heart is through his crotch, and don't ever forget it."

"I do not think I will need that piece of information, Becca," sighs Ulli, falling asleep.

Becca has seen Gerry. They have "opened negotiations," as Gerry calls it. He and Angel appear one afternoon while Becca is waxing her legs. She sits stiffly in the living room, peeling off bits of wax, like one of Ulli's martyrs.

"Becca, you know that makes me sick," Gerry says.

"I don't shave anymore, Becca. I'm liberated," Angel confesses, lifting one perfect leg and swinging it over Gerry's lap.

Gerry pats it happily. "I can't find some notes I need for a paper, Becca. I thought maybe I'd take a look in the attic."

"Did you know Ulli is dying?" Becca asks him coldly, blocking his passage to the stairs.

"Dying?"

"Yep." Becca has not previously admitted this to herself but feels the need to swiftly punish them both.

"John said she was very sick, but . . ."

"He's very articulate, your friend John."

"You should know, Becca. I hear you're fucking John."
Gerry glares at her across the bannister.

"Where the hell did you hear that? That's a lie!"

"Well, maybe you should, Becca, you look lonely," says
Gerry and pats her on the arm.

Becca swallows, rolling the little balls of wax in her hand.
She can hear Angel talking to the girls on the front porch.

"And you don't have to wait for the weekends. You can
come out anytime you want and ride."

"Horses!" sigh Alexy and Tory, happily.

Oh, God, thinks Becca, how can I compete with a horse?

"What are you looking for?" Becca asks Tory, who is
squinting into the phone book. Maybe she needs to have her
eyes tested, thinks Becca, guiltily.

"It's the new one. I want to make sure they got our names
spelled right."

"Are we there?" Becca peeks over her shoulder.

"Hey! They listed Daddy twice. Look! Once with you and
once with Angel."

Becca stares in horror. "You're slobbering apple all over
the S's, Victoria," she says.

"My name is Tory." She flips through the pages. "Got a
pencil, Mommy?"

"Here . . . what are you doing?"

"Crossing out Ulli's name," she says busily.

"Oh, Tory," Becca cries. She remembers Tory at the age
of five. " 'Can't we just play with them until they die?' "

"What?"

"I was thinking about something that happened when
you were a little, little girl. Some baby robins fell out of a
nest in the garage and we put them in a box with a towel on
the bottom, but I could see they couldn't survive. So I

explained to you why mother birds kick babies out of the
nest, and that it would be more humane for me to suffocate
them quickly, because they didn't have a chance. And you
looked up at me and asked, 'But couldn't we just play with
them until they die?' "

"I did not! I never said such a dumb thing!" Tory objects,
stamping her foot.

But Becca can tell her daughter is pleased she was so
tough.

"Becca! *Kom hit!*"

Becca runs down the stairs into the kitchen. Ulli is
speaking Swedish more and more frequently these days.
She finds her hanging onto a counter, shaking violently. "I
. . . IIII'm having a seizure. . . ."

"What do I do?" Becca screams.

"Dooo . . . not let me . . ." Ulli falls heavily, just catching
one of Becca's outstretched arms. They both tumble to the
floor.

"It is over," she announces. "A short one, Becca." She is
leaning on her, trying to catch her breath.

"What can I do?" Becca asks over and over. Ulli looks so
terrible, her features white and badly distorted.

"I should be in bed. Get John to carry me."

"He's not here, he took the kids to buy a pumpkin. Oh,
please Ulli, tell me how to make you better."

"Call the hospital, Becca."

Becca dials the phone shakily, her voice cracking in
imitation of Ulli's. She shouts at the person on the other
end.

"Do you think you can walk upstairs?" asks Becca, hanging up the phone.

Ulli shakes her head on one side, like a swimmer dripping
water from an ear. "There is no feeling in my whole side,
Becca . . . I do not think so. . . ."

"Okay," breathes Becca and bends over, not at all sure where to begin. She arranges Ulli's arms around her neck and scoops her up.

"Becca," Ulli objects lightly.

"Shh, I'm strong enough," says Becca, carrying her.

Ulli is very light, lighter than either of her daughters, she is sure. Becca carries her up the stairs. Like Rhett Butler, she thinks crazily.

This strength must be all men have over women: this propensity for women to collapse against men, to mold their soft yielding bodies into the harder planes of men. One party falls, the other picks up: the long historical dance of the sexes.

"Ulli, how many men have you slept with?" Becca asks.

"Ah, Becca, what questions!"

"In college, we used to sit around forever and play a game called Truth. Everyone had to tell the most private thing about themselves. Something they had never revealed before." It is probably Ulli's hospital room that makes her think of it. Becca is curled up on the other bed in the moist overheated air. "Am I making you tired, Ulli?"

"Ah, no. I love to have you here, Becca, but you must do some other things, too."

"The children are in school all day. What would I do?"

"Did you peruse the course in ballet you might teach?"

" 'Peruse'? Oh, Ulli, you mean 'pursue,' " laughs Becca.

"Ah, well, did you?"

"Ulli, I can't even teach five-year-olds. I haven't taken a class in years." She smooths Ulli's pillow, trying not to look at her white fingernails.

"Do you want to know how many men I sleep with?"

"I was just joking, Ulli."

"Soon I will have to play Truth with God, Becca, it is not so bad to practice now. Do not make a face, it is the facts. I have slept with . . ."

"Oh, my God, folks, she's still counting!"

"It is very hard for me to count, Becca."

"I'm sorry."

"Let me see, there is John and a man I loved. I think I really loved, Becca, he was a painter in Paris, Hungarian. Ah, I do not remember his names. And a writer in New York, a famous man. It was very bad, Becca, he was married and I was very jealous and very guilty . . . did I say John?"

"Don't forget Lars."

"Ah, Lars. I saw him last night. Last night I saw my whole life, Becca. That is very common when one is . . ." Ulli shrugs. "But I thought it would be like a movie. No, it was like a little cartoon book I had once. *Kalle Anka* . . . Donald Duck," she translates. "It has a slightly different picture on each page, so if you flip through it fast, the pictures move. That is how it went . . . flip, flip. My whole life."

Becca holds Ulli's good hand. "Ulli, this summer I slept with a man in France."

"I hope it was nice for you, Becca."

"He was a Swede, Ulli and . . ."

"*Jo?*" Ulli is closing her eyes.

"I thought it was you making love to me," says Becca.

"Becca, don't . . ."

"Ulli, I must tell you how much I love you," starts Becca but ends up looking out the window, also.

"I am too tired to play Truth," says Ulli, dropping her hand.

One rainy afternoon, Becca paints Ulli's toenails. Red. She lifts the stiff sheets and finds Ulli's feet, long and thin as an ivory crucifix.

"What are you doing now?" asks the nurse, with the next round of medication, grabbing the bottle from Becca's hand. "Now, look." Little drops of polish, like Snow White's blood in Alexy's book, fall onto the sheets.

"I thought it would be nice. She was so beautiful," Becca sighs sadly.

"How do you expect us to tell if the blood is circulating?" asks the nurse, rubbing Ulli's toenail with alcohol.

"That's a helluva scientific method!" Becca shouts, slamming the door. But she goes into the ladies' room to check out her own.

"Ah, Becca, how funny!" Ulli says, when she awakens. "I think I have found a place worse than the convent," she whispers.

"Bitches!"

"You must not be so hard. It is a very tough job, I think."

" 'And I still believe people are basically good at heart,' " Becca lisps like Little Becca did for Grandpops' radio spots.

"Who says that, Becca?"

"Anne Frank."

"Ah, *jo.*"

"There wasn't a little Jewish girl of my generation who wasn't totally terrified and intimidated by that diary, the play, the film . . ."

"*Jo,* it is very sad."

"Sad! I kept thinking, what if I had perished and they had found my diary? God, do you know what kind of junk I wrote when I was sixteen? Why was she so fucking articulate?"

"You do not know how you would have behaved, Becca."

"If you recall, I'm not very brave."

"Sometimes situations bring out things in people they do not know they have. You are always putting yourself down, Becca. Is that the expression? You do not know what you are like at all." She digs her hand into Becca's arm. "Ugh!" she moans.

"Does it hurt?" Becca cries, holding Ulli's hand.

"No, no, it is okay now. It is like during labor, Becca. I remember during the worst part of it I feel as if I can leave my body and stand outside of it. Watching, it does not hurt so."

Becca wrinkles her forehead so she will not cry. This trick, of course, is what Ulli took from the convent. Ulli's soul is a neatly wrapped package, a smooth kernel, all of one piece, while Becca's is like the chocolate in a marble cake. It swirls messily through her healthy body, lumping in her ovaries, her brain, mostly in her aching heart.

"What are you guys doing in there?" asks Becca, knocking on the door to the playroom.

"Playing Life," says Alexy.

Is this some new version of Doctor? They are getting too old for this kind of stuff, thinks Becca and pushes open the door.

"The Game of Life," sighs Alexy. "Daddy bought it for us last weekend."

"He would," Becca smirks. Gerry would love to reduce life to a board game. "Hi, Christoph," she smiles cheerfully, although he continues to stare at the printed rules. "Can I play? I'm dying to play Life," says Becca, and crossing her legs, sits in one neat motion on the floor.

The children stare at her. Becca hates to play games; she has just screamed at them to go to the playroom and leave her alone. But they are too polite to say no. Tory hands her a little car and plunks a pick into it.

"Oh, no," Becca groans, "pink for girls and blue for boys."

"It's just a game, Mommy," Tory warns.

"I know. I'm sorry. I didn't really want to play. I just wanted to look at it. What happens at the end?" Becca pushes a finger down the squiggly path, looking for hospitals, respirators, funeral homes, a plastic hearse for the long ride to the cemetery.

"Nothing happens," Alexy informs her impatiently. "Someone wins. Then it's over."

A vast improvement over the real thing, thinks Becca, closing the door behind her.

At Ulli's request, Becca is reading aloud from *The Diary of Anne Frank*. A strange choice, the selection of an adolescent, but Ulli is retreating farther and farther away. The book is more beautiful than Becca could have remembered, she is touched and astounded by this beauty. She will give the book to one of her daughters soon, but which one? The one who thinks she may stop breathing any minute, or the daughter who insists she will live forever?

Oh, Grandma Rosie, thinks Becca, there is no need for an onion in your bodice when there is life going on. She closes the book; Ulli has fallen asleep.

"Once upon a time," Becca begins, "a little princess was born in Chicago. Her grandfather was the King of Cadillacs on the South Side. The birth was hailed as a great event and from all over the city her fairy *tantes,* with their perms and open-toe pumps and short veils and painted fingernails, assembled. They wished her curly hair and straight teeth and big breasts and a nice voice and a mink coat. Someone donated a foolproof cheesecake recipe. 'Diamonds are a girl's best friend,' offered another.

"Suddenly the princess' parents burst into the showroom with their gift: reality! They wanted her to do well in school and keep her legs crossed at the ankles and be a credit to them and their neighborhood.

"Luckily, when the princess grew up she met Ulli the good witch of the North. 'Ah, Becca,' the good witch would sigh, 'I think this is the best life.' "

" 'Somewhere over the rainbow, way up high,' " Becca sings for sleeping Ulli, " 'there's a land that I've heard of once in a lullaby. . . .' "

When she finishes singing, she looks up to see two nurses, a resident, and John, some of them crying.

Five

With Ulli home from the hospital, Becca takes her daughters to visit her parents for Christmas vacation. In the spirit of their generation, they have recently moved to Florida. Becca knows she is tolerated for old-times' sake, for appearance, as a chaperone for The Grandchildren. Her parents and she have long maintained a relationship resembling a square dance: It called for a previous knowledge of the steps, the prodding of a faceless caller, and the reassurance that one will not be stuck with one's own partner too often or for too long.

"Is that all you have to wear?" Becca's mother greets her at the airport, her new face-lift dropping. "You look like a bunch of farmers." She walks past Becca and grabs Alexy and Tory. "How you've grown!" she begins.

"Where's Daddy?"

Becca's father is circling the jammed airport in pursuit of a parking space, a man on a holy search.

"Daddy's outside, Becca, we'll go tell him you're here. You bring the luggage. . . ." Her mother bustles the girls out the door, whispering to them. "I have a little surprise for you, hidden away. . . ."

Becca stares after her mother, the wicked witch of her childhood. Maybe affection needs to skip a generation, like intelligence and domesticity.

Becca's father has been reborn as the hustle king of the Country Club. A man whose skin she would have sworn was worsted and charcoal gray dresses now in fruit colors. In fact, the only thing that has not changed about him is his intense lack of interest in Becca's problems. Quite frankly, he is head-over-heels in love with himself, with his full head of silver hair, with his slim feet cast in fine Italian shoes, his strong arms covered by cashmere golf sweaters, his firm fanny tucked into linen trousers. Every morning, he lovingly shaves in his Time Man of the Year mirror, a Father's Day gift from Alexy and Tory, and slips a gold chain around his neck, with the Hebrew letter, *chei,* hanging from it.

"Life!" he bellows at Becca. "It means 'life'! Stop that, Alexy!"

Alexy is pushing the button for the automatic windows up and down.

"Goddamn it, the air conditioning's on. Make her stop that, Rebecca. One of them is going to lose a finger."

"Make the ceiling open, Joey," orders Tory.

"Becca, could you ask her please to call me 'Grandpa' or 'Grandfather' or something. Not 'Joey.' "

"You may speak directly to her, Daddy. She speaks English."

"Your mother used to call her grandfather 'Grand-pops,' " says her mother, wedged happily in the back seat between her granddaughters.

"I loved him so much," sighs Becca.

"He spoiled you rotten, Becca," says her father.

"He may have ruined your life," adds her mother. "He gave you unrealistic expectations about men." Becca's mother is doing psychology at the Dade County Adult School.

"We never discussed men," says Becca, sadly.

"One more time!" shouts her father at the children, and with the flick of a manicured finger, the sunroof opens and closes like a device useful in a Greek tragedy.

"Why don't we have a Cadillac?" asks Tory.

"She's driving a Mercedes these days," smirks Alexy.

"Don't call your mother 'she,' " corrects Joey, and without missing a beat, "Where'd you get a Mercedes, Becca?"

"It's Ulli's. Gerry took our car, so . . ." Becca has a headache already. She has been in Florida for fifteen minutes so far.

"How is Ulli?" asks Becca's mother. She approves of her highly, has been in her house and admired its odor and order.

"She's dying," Tory replies.

"She is very sick," corrects Becca. "Right now, she's quite well, actually."

"Well, she's dying. Everybody knows that but her . . . Rebecca over there," giggles Tory.

"Are we rich?" asks Alexy. "Is Grandpops rich? Is Christoph rich?" The sociologist's daughter wishes to classify everybody immediately.

"When you grow up you can be very rich and drive Cadillacs and embarrass the shit out of me, okay?"

"Watch your language in my car, madame!" bellows Joey.

* * *

They eat in a McDonald's housed in a fake hacienda. In the midst of a real tropical paradise, the plants in this McDonald's are plastic. In one corner, a purple-haired woman chews a Big Mac very, very slowly, only her lips chomping slightly, the rest of her face as rigid as a cheap Halloween mask.

"Lousy face-lift," Becca's mother explains. She pulls back her fluffy gray bangs to reveal a row of tiny yellow marks like tick bites.

"Oh, Mother, what was wrong with your old face?" asks Becca.

"Just you wait, Becca. I hope to God that I am around to hear you change your tune when your face is hanging six inches lower than it used to." She emits the sighing cluck that accompanied most of Becca's youthful comings and goings. "You don't look too bad. As soon as I can sort you out . . ."

Oh, that expression! Becca as a child imagined herself as the joker, a piece of bent card, in a particularly sticky deck.

"Look what Grandma Judy gave us!" Tory shoves a doll in Becca's face. "Barbie dolls!" she sneers triumphantly.

Becca stares at Ken and Barbie, plastic lovers, her mother's little surprise. For years, she had held out against them, not just for political reasons, but aesthetic ones as well. She watches Ken in swimming trunks and Barbie in a dangerously flimsy negligee wade through a puddle of chocolate shakes and straddle a few French fries. If Ken and Barbie have grandparents, they live right here, she thinks, in the Mañana Adult Community.

"I just love that, 'Adult Community,' " says Becca as they drive through the front gates, past the fountains that play music and display all the colors of the rainbow. "As if the rest of us are wandering around in a gigantic kindergarten."

"It refers to the fact," says her father, always ready to enlighten her, "that there are no children allowed."

"It's against the law?" asks Becca, amused.

"Against the law," breathes Tory, and Alexy moves closer to Becca.

Becca wanders through the new house, the color of citrus fruit, like an amnesiac, looking for clues of a former life. "Weren't you gray?" she asks the orange chairs in the dining room. She knows the yellow love seat was maroon. "Where did you put the breakfront?"

"We sold that, Becca."

"You sold the breakfront?" That was Becca's favorite piece of furniture, filled with painted china people: drunken sailors and balloon women, graceful geishas and curtseying shepherdesses; she used it as a dollhouse. When her mother was out playing bridge or mah-jongg, depending upon the day of the week, Becca, alone with the dozing maid, would rearrange the shelves, making new lives for the inhabitants. She would reunite sisters, allow a damsel in distress some comfort from an older man.

"I thought you hated our furniture, Becca," says her mother.

"Oh, the *tsores* you gave your mother, Becca, turning up your nose at everything. 'Less is more,' you used to say."

"And '*quel* junk!' Do you remember that, Joey? That was another of her favorite expressions."

"Did you really want the breakfront, Becca?"

"Well, ah, no, I guess not, really," sighs Becca.

Becca accompanies her parents golfing. She sits in the back of the little cart, hopefully hidden by the bags of clubs. She is afraid this solo appearance has been commanded so they may discuss Gerry. In the last few days, Becca has come to understand that she is the only Jewish daughter of her generation without two cars, a set of Vuitton luggage, Sherle Wagner bathroom fixtures, four sons preparing for their Bar Mitzvahs and a husband. National statistics withstanding, only one of the Schumans' friends' children has been . . . (the word "divorced" is whispered here), and she remarried immediately and a heart surgeon.

Watching her parents play golf, Becca experiences a strong feeling of *déjà vu*. How's that for a board game? she asks the absent Gerry, although she knows *déjà vu* is more the province of the psychologist and the poet. But Becca has been here before.

"Last night I saw my whole life in front of me," Ulli had said to Becca in the hospital. Flip, flip.

Becca was eight, nine, and sitting in a sand trap, making a colored forest with tees from a suede drawstring bag. Her mother was shouting and running back and forth, following her father over the greens, in a ridiculous kilt and brown-and-white shoes with flapping tassels. Becca stared at those knees. which were not exposed frequently and were red and round as apples.

Why was she with them? She usually spent Saturdays with her grandparents, stretching dough and practicing dance routines.

"Would you at least get her out of that sand trap, Judith? I don't know why you had to drag her along. She'll probably have her head cracked open and my mother won't speak to us again."

"That'll be a blessing!" her mother screamed.

Becca stares at her mother's knees now, her stringy tanned legs. Both her parents are so tanned they are as creased as origami. They seem a separate race, truly one of the lost tribes.

"Hand me a five iron, Becca?" her father asks.

"Which one is that?"

"They have numbers on them. Just read, Becca," he says

impatiently.

"Is it one of the ones with a little hat?"

"Where did you grow up?" he asks, pulling out his own club.

"Did you ever take me golfing when I was a little girl?"

"I doubt it," says her mother, repairing her lipstick. "You spent every Saturday with Grandma Rosie and Grandpops."

"It made it very nice for you, Judith. That my parents were so available."

"Available! I was hardly allowed near her. When I came back from Texas they wouldn't let me have her for a month!"

"Judith, I can't concentrate." Her father swings and misses.

"Following you all over the damn country from army base to army base, keeping an eye on you and your women!" Her mother is trying to cry; there are no tears. "It hurts to cry, you know that, Joey!" The surgeon has mistakenly closed most of her tear ducts.

"Stop, please stop!" Becca says, covering her ears, hiding her face in the red cowhide of her mother's bag. Becca has accumulated and assimilated enough facts about her childhood; she has found the pieces that fit, her story is functional. If she has to rewrite her grandparents as the villains and her mother as an unsung heroine, it won't work.

When she raises her head, her mother is standing on a little mound of grass, slamming an orange ball 150 yards down the fairway.

"I didn't know. . ." says Becca to her father.

"Next time, please release the brake before you attempt to drive the cart," he tells her.

At night, Becca sneaks out of the house and swims naked in the country-club pool. She peels off her big terry robe, carefully looking around for anyone, and dives directly into the deepest end. The water, warm, chlorinated, laps into her injured crevices, cradles her breasts. Rising alone and shiny from the shallow end, she imagines Grandpops reclining on a chaise lounge, smoking a big cigar, applauding, as he did on visiting days at camp.

"So, *nu*, Becca, what's a matter?"

"Oh, hi, Grandpops."

"You will catch your death . . . *oy*, Becca, cover up your *pupik*, you are naked as a chicken." He pushes his straw boater down over one eye.

"Oh, Grandpops, they say you ruined me. That I will never find a man who will love me the way you did."

"Forget men, Becca, they don't make them the way they used to." He bangs his cane against his shoe and tosses his hat in the air. "Hey, Becca, did you hear about the 72-year-old man who marries the 18-year-old girl?"

"No, Grandpops, what about the 72-year-old man who marries the 18-year-old girl?"

"I'm glad you asked that! Well, he does." He crosses his legs and leans on his cane. "About two months later, she finds out he's fooling around with a 65-year-old woman. Well, the little wifey comes to him and says, 'What does she have that I don't have?' 'Patience!' he says!"

But no one came, only an occasional adolescent, a wayward grandchild sent down while his parents skied at Gstaad or sunned at St. Thomas, another fugitive from authority, rolling a joint near the ping-pong room. Much as she would have liked to join him, Becca knows that age has turned her into the enemy.

Becca dries herself and walks through the soft humid silence, broken only by the occasional clink of backgammon pieces or the sound of a TV on someone's screened-in porch; one night, she imagines she hears John's voice. Home safe, she sneaks into the huge avocado colored freezer and steals two chocolate ice cream sandwiches, eats them alone in her bedroom, the guest room, and presses her sticky fingers between her damp thighs, searching for the root of her problem.

Becca dreams about Ulli. She dreams Ulli is her mother and takes her by the hand on the elevated train downtown to the ballet studio, where she had started dancing. She dreams she and Ulli are a vaudeville team, dressed in striped blazers and straw boaters. They lean on gold-tipped canes.

"How do you do, Mr. Fine?" asks Ulli.

"Okey-dokey, Mr. Olsen. How are you?"

"I am fine."

"No, no, you're Olsen, I'm Fine!" Becca cackles, then shouts, "I'm fine! I'm fine!"

Ulli is back in the hospital after only two weeks. Becca calls the house nightly, sometimes speaking to the new housekeeper, sometimes John. "It's just a precaution," says John, in his even broadcaster's voice. "Ulli's *fine*, Becca."

What can she say? No, she's Olsen, I'm Fine.

Becca sits at the pool in lotus position, watching her daughters make friends, under the warm gaze of men: the big fleshy hairy men she grew up appreciating, men with thick black pompadours and fat pieces of gold jewelry, inheritors of successful businesses, or an occasional son-in-law in the medical profession, dangling thick paperbacks by Harold Robbins, driving golf carts with pink-and-white canopies. There is a gaggle of wives, too, many pregnant but well-groomed, most oiled like basting chickens. In the pool, the men's arms brush against Becca's breasts.

She goes out for dinner with the son of a friend of her parents, a large friendly man named Larry who is between tiny wives and manufactures mattresses. Sliding timidly into the car, Becca is reminded of a dozen strange front seats, rubbing against big shoulders, guessing desires from male profiles: ear, one nostril with a few hairs, maybe a mole, a square jaw. She has not been on a date in years.

Larry orders for both of them, Beef Wellington and a chilled Moselle. "I like white wine," he tells Becca so she will know he knows the difference.

Becca discovers she cannot drink white wine with steak; she opts for the wine.

In his big car, parked in front of her parents' lime-green house, Becca moves close to him, sits on his lap, wraps her arms around his thick neck, hugs him like a favorite teddy. "I have a secret," she whispers.

"Yeah?" he asks politely.

"I swim nude every night."

"Where?"

"The Club. Really. Come on, I'll show you."

He stands on the diving board, as Becca removes her clothes, hands them to him, dives neatly into the pool.

"Larry," she whispers, pulling herself out and wringing out her hair. "Fuck me."

"Becca. Now?"

"Now!"

"Where? On the shuffleboard court, maybe?" He pulls away. "Hey, Becca, you're getting my Guccis wet."

Larry and Becca play doubles with their fathers; his father, daring layers of flesh and sweat, Becca's, slim and stiff. Like Jimmy Connors, Becca's father carries several racquets.

Under their melting eyes, Becca soars, plays better than she ever has, lobbing, slamming, running madly, flying over their balding heads. Becca is positively blooming down here.

In the clubhouse for lunch, Larry's father takes the space of flesh between her halter and her tennis skirt and squeezes. "Nice girl," he announces, as if she were a giant mango. "She should have a nice husband."

"She has a nice husband," Becca's father says, adjusting his bifocals.

"I do not. He's a shmuck."

"Oooh, she has a dirty mouth, your daughter, Joey," the other man says, amused. "I like that," he announces and strokes her upper arm. "Don't you, Larry?"

"If it goes with other things," Larry says, pleasantly, picking his father's menu off the floor.

"Ho, ho," explodes the old man. "Some boy I've got, right Joey? Huh, sweetheart?"

Becca lifts her eyebrows and smirks across the table. The waitress, a big blond girl with braces on her teeth and loose heavy breasts like Angel's, stands over them on one hip.

Larry ignores Becca. "What are you going to eat, Pop?" He pinches the waitress. "So what's not good to eat?"

The last night Becca is in Florida, they all go to the Country Club for the Thursday night buffet, a feast so great it must be measured in distance: The Mile Long Banquet. Alexy and Tory move right into this citrus society, dressed in identical long checked dresses and pinafores, patent-leather Mary Janes, their hair neatly braided with matching ribbons, piling their plates with food more exotic than the couscous and cassoulets of their academic childhoods. Watching them two-stepping with Larry and his father to "Fly Me to the Moon," Becca tries to remember what they looked like in overalls and boots on the farm, or in yellow macs and school socks and caps. Poor little girls, thinks Becca, hopping cultures like mud puddles.

"What are you thinking about?" Larry asks, dancing with Becca.

"A multiple-choice lifestyles test for my daughters," she sighs.

His arm loosens like all those lovely arms used to in high

school. "I think you're too smart for me, Becca."

"I'm just verbal," Becca assures him.

"My father wants to know if you're good in bed."

"Logical question for a mattress manufacturer," says Becca. "The Jewish princess and the pea."

Becca and her father slow-dance to a big band medley. "You going tomorrow?" he asks, taking her hand.

"Is tomorrow soon enough?" she asks, twirling under his arm.

"Why don't you let the girls stay longer? Mother's crazy about them."

"But not me, huh?" The tempo changes to a jitterbug. Whew, can he dance! Becca has forgotten that he too is the descendent of Henry B. Schlag Schuman's softshoes.

"She says you swim alone after we've gone to bed. That's against Club rules. Also," he attempts to flip Becca over one hip and then the other, "without a suit."

"How does she know that?" Grabbing her father's hands, she slides on her back through his opened arthritic knees.

"You leave footprints all over the linoleum and your suit's dry."

"Wow! She's some detective, my mother." Becca remembers her mother sniffing blouses for cigarette smoke, inspecting panties for traces of semen.

He opens his arm and, taking Becca's, promenades her around the dance floor. Quite a crowd has gathered, there are only a few couples left. The band switches to a cha-cha-cha.

"One . . . two . . . three, one-two-three," Becca's father whispers fiercely. "What the hell did they teach at Bennington?"

"I didn't study ballroom dancing at Bennington, Daddy. CHA-CHA-CHA!" Becca and her father sidestep around each other, clapping one, two, three.

"You're leading on Larry Gold. You're going to get in

trouble."

"Oh, boy, have the times changed. My father's worried about preserving the virtue of people's sons these days!"

"I'm warning you as an attorney, Becca, not just as your father." He spins her around and around."And." The final sin. "You left the freezer door open last night!" he announces triumphantly, taking a deep bow.

Suddenly, everyone is applauding and a bald grinning man shoves a large plastic silver trophy into Becca's hands. "And first prize in the freestyle goes to Joey Schuman and his daughter RAbecca!"

Six

"You bastard! You son of a bitch!" Becca screams before she is even into the house. "Why didn't you tell me? You just let me march in there like Little Red Riding Hood!"

John looks up, surprised. He is standing in the living room, putting away a massive aluminum Christmas tree. "I've laid out all the pieces in order, Becca, so don't start . . ."

"What is that?"

"My tree. I've always wanted to get one, but Ulli wouldn't let me."

"An aluminum tree in her house? Oh, God, I don't believe you, you son of a bitch, you couldn't wait for her to die!" She kicks around some silver limbs. "You want Ulli to die!"

"Becca, shut up, everyone can hear you. Christoph is upstairs. . . ."

"You're going to let her die. You can't do this, Ulli can't die!" Becca picks up the fireplace tongs and comes after John, swinging it dangerously near his face. He grabs her efficiently around her thighs and tackles her so that she falls smack against the metal rim of the glass coffee table.

"Aw!" Becca screams. "Ah!" she screams again, tasting the first of her blood that is pouring down her chin.

John stares at her. "Jesus God, Becca, I didn't mean to . . . your lip, oh God. . . ."

Becca brings her hand up to her mouth, but comes away with too much blood. "My teeth still there?" she asks, trying not to swallow. She raises her hand and imagines there is a piece of her lip in it.

"Just lie still, Becca. I mean it," John warns. "I'm going to get some ice."

But Becca pulls herself up on the edge of the table and, in the glass, catches a blurred image, a Munch lithograph: her teeth floating in a sea of red.

"What the hell are you doing, Becca? I told you not to move!"

"I just wanted to check out my teeth, my father spent a small fortune on them."

"You can really talk, can't you? Jesus Christ, Becca, shut up," he says quietly, bending close to her, blotting her face with paper towels. "We'd better go to the hospital, it's a big cut." He looks down. "God, I feel sick about this. . . ."

"Oh, goody, the hospital. I just came from there. Maybe Ulli and I can be roomies."

"Becca, please."

"Well, what happened to you?" asks the orderly in the emergency room, friendly as a counterboy at McDonald's.

"We were having a little predinner game of football," says Becca.

"Wow! Hey, are you two married?" he laughs, checking the chart.

"Who's your doctor, Mrs. Solomon?" the nurse inquires efficiently.

"Hold my hand, please," Becca asks John.

Maybe Becca imagines it, she is woozy from medication, but there is a change in Ulli since this afternoon. There appears to be even less color in her face, and now another IV drips silently into the other arm.

Ulli lifts herself with difficulty, balancing on an elbow. "What happened to you?"

"Oh, it's my do-it-yourself plastic surgery kit," says Becca, heartily. "I'm putting my nose back the way it was." She holds Ulli's plugged hand.

"I . . ." John sways back and forth on his wing tips.

"I slipped on the rug and fell into the coffee table."

"Poor Becca."

"You know what a terrific dancer I am. 'Meringue toes' they called me at Bennington." Becca wipes some tears away. She tries to read the bottle; what is this stuff dripping into Ulli?

"John," Ulli says wearily, "you must move the table and put things away. Wrap them up. Becca, would you like the little teapot with the hearts?"

Becca sees the pot tipping back and forth a hundred times in their friendship; one of Ulli's hands on the handle, one on the top.

"Becca? Becca?" says Ulli, squeezing her hand a little. "Ah, Becca, does it hurt so much?"

"What hurt?"

"Your lip, Becca. You have not stopped crying since you walked in here."

* * *

Becca cannot stop crying. She cries walking down the hospital steps, she cries in John's car. When he lifts her and carries her into his house, she pauses, but for once does not make an obvious easy joke. John sits down on the Barcelona chairs with Becca on his lap and she sobs against his smooth shirt. Sobs out everything, all the hurts: Ulli, Gerry, her daughters' thoughtless puberty, her parents' fickle retirement.

"Oh, Becca, don't cry," John says, stroking her hair. "You'll open the stitches."

"I have to cry. Shit, everything is so wrong. Everything." She puts her head down on his chest, then smiles crookedly. "I almost put my thumb in my mouth."

"You're such a child, Becca," laughs John.

"That's just what Ulli would say, 'Vot a child!' "

"Oh, Becca," says John, in horror. "Don't!"

"I'm sorry," she apologizes and puts her arms around his neck and kisses him on the mouth.

John turns, embraces her passionately, starts to remove her clothes, like peeling the skin from an almond.

"Oh, God, John, no!" Becca whispers, trying to pull away from him. "Please, stop."

"Becca, I need this, please," he pleads, undressing himself swiftly, settling her uneasily across the chairs.

"No, John, think of Ulli, and the children . . . what if Christopher comes downstairs. What will I say to Ulli?" she cries.

John stares down at her, blindly, as if she is babbling in foreign tongues. A madwoman. He ignores her mumbling and lifts her legs over his shoulders.

"John . . . uh," Becca whispers. Finally, she understands that this has nothing to do with sex, this is pure white flashing need. So she lies back, Victorian in her patience and submission, determined out of loyalty to Ulli to feel nothing, take nothing from this moment. But it is too late to be passive. Becca has been taking this trip for too long, she has imagined this for many years and must cry out and move and moan, grab her own desire. Over John's left shoulder, she sees Christopher in the doorway, taking a huge bite out of an apple.

Seven

On an early spring day, Becca is opening the wide glass doors to the hospital for her daily visit to Ulli. It is the kind of day they would gather children and picnic things and find a piece of earth to hold them. They would talk of gardens and summer plans. Nothing in the coming attractions has prepared Becca for the horror film that is playing at her local theatre.

Becca is taking a picnic, balancing a loaded basket on one arm, swinging a thermos from the other. These are her magic totems to coax Ulli back to the land of the living. Rebecca Schuman, age twelve and breathless, sat in the dusty balcony of the Shubert Theatre for three solid weeks watching Ann Bancroft as Annie Sullivan civilize Patty

Duke's Helen Keller. Every day Becca waits like the Miracle Worker for the right moment. Patience, advised Grandpops.

The nurses, unseeing and unfeeling, ignore Becca as she tiptoes down the corridor on woven espadrilles. A nurse stationed in a chair in the corner of Ulli's room sighs, closes her magazine and exits; she has caught this act before.

"Well, Ulli," says Becca. "Great day for a picnic!"

Ulli lies silently on the bed, the sheet arranged perfectly folded up to her armpits, tucked in on both sides; her hands are flat, palms down, the nails bleached whiter than snow. A silk robe is spread uselessly at the foot of the bed. Tubes, like exotic bracelets, decorate her pale arms, attached to plastic bubbles that hang precariously from ceiling hooks. They have performed surgery again, and Ulli sports a gauze turban. Blond fuzz is beginning to sprout from an opening in the bandage.

"I brought you some raspberries," says Becca, crazily, spreading a checkered cloth on the swinging bed tray. She knows Ulli has had no solid food for at least a month, but assumes she is waiting for the right combination of things. Becca pulls out a tiny whisk, originally from a toy set of Alexy's, and whips cream in the plastic ice pitcher, chatting away.

"I signed all the kids up for tennis for the spring session. Just wait until you play with Christoph, he is really good, Ulli." Becca nods for both of them and spreads paté on thin slices of toast, fashioning a sunflower from a cornichon, one of Ulli's own tricks. "Paté, Ulli?"

Suddenly, Becca strikes the food off the tray with the back of her arm. "Ulli!" she screams. "Wake up! Stop this, please! Fuck the Sleeping Beauty act!" Becca climbs on the bed and kneels, grabbing the tops of Ulli's thighs. "Listen to me, you've got to stop this and help me. Gerry's out there on that farm, screwing Angelica and shoveling manure. Hey, come on, Ulli, that's worth a million laughs, Gerry's finally shoveling real shit! And John." She crawls further up the bed and pulls at one of Ulli's doll arms. "You remember good old John. John is living with me these days, in my house and in my bed, Ulli. Ulli! John is in my bed!" Becca is sobbing on Ulli's broken chest. At last, she slaps Ulli across the face. Her fingers leave deep blue welts on Ulli's crystal jaw.

Ulli sits up rigidly, straight as a ladder-back chair, her blue eyes snap open. "*Mama*," she says in a delicate lisp, "*vill du gå med på badstrand?*" Then she falls back, as if knocked over.

"Nurse!" screams Becca, clambering down from the bed, running down the halls. "Nurse! Come immediately! You must come!"

Lights flash, buzzers ring and, flapping down the hall like a peagreen penguin, comes Becca's gynecologist in his surgical gown and slippers. "Well, well, Mrs. Solomon."

He grabs her under the elbow, as if escorting her across a dangerous intersection, and steers her down the hallway, gesturing to various uniformed people who silently join them, as in a folk dance. "How are you, Becca?"

"Oh, Dr. Nelson, I am glad to see you. Ulli is down the hall and she is very sick, and . . ."

A big dark man comes up behind her and takes the other elbow so that they lift her slightly off the ground. She has to flex her toes to keep her shoes from falling off. Swinging her, they bring her into a darkened room.

"There, there, Becca. Just lie back, that's a good girl, don't fight me, and I'm going to give you a little shot, just a pinprick. . . ."

The other man is holding her down, across her shoulders.

"Look, I think you have the wrong patient, Ulli's very sick. . . ."

"That's a good girl, just hold still. . . ."

When she awakens, she is in her bed at home. Gerry and John stand together at the end, as solid as her grandmother's brass Sabbath candlesticks. Who took her home? Whom did they call? "Would you stop laughing for chrissake," snaps Gerry. "You're behaving as if you're watching a cartoon." "No, not a cartoon, this is more like a Mozart opera," Becca objects. "Husbands and lovers, people popping out of closets and being dragged into dark rooms. Oh, God!" Her eyes are filled with tears. "Get out of here, both of you!" she hisses between her teeth.

They move towards the door at the same moment, in relief, stepping out of the way for each other ("After you, Alphonse. No, no, after you, Gaston," went a routine Grandpops had taught Becca), until they are both stuck in the door. "Pure Mozart!" she screams from under the covers. Only without the beautiful music.

Sometimes Ulli and Becca went to the opera in New York. Ulli taught Becca about couplets and motifs. "Becca," she would say, "in Wagner's *Die Fliegende Holländer*, Senata sits, virginal, but not spinning, waiting for the legendary Dutchman."

But Ulli is on the beach at Saltsjöbaden, and Becca is under the covers. She wraps the sheet around her and trips sleepily down the hall to her daughters' room. She lies down on the scratchy rug that separates their narrow beds and takes a breath between each of theirs. They mumble poetry in their sleep. The men's voices float up through the floor: deep, harsh, serious. She pounds down the stairs.

"What are you talking about?" asks Becca, opening the door to the study.

"Spain," John says roughly and lights a cigarette.

"Spain!" Becca spits. "Spain!" She cries in disbelief. God,

men are so far from the stuff of life there is no hope for them. They are always stuck in the quicksand of someone else's reality.

The two men look away, tap their big feet, drink some cognac, light cigarettes and pipes, embarrassed for each other by her behavior. Each blushes for the other, to think she had belonged to him.

Becca looks at the large lump in her bed; it is John. Had the men merely shaken hands at the foot of her bed? "Be my guest," said Gerry. "Thanks, old man," said John. Oh, God, has it come to this? The rights to her body have been officially transferred over brandy and cigars in the middle of the night.

Cautiously, Becca observes this handsome creature: his big head with carefully styled hair, thick and barely mussed. She moves the sheet off his body so she may view the merchandise more carefully. She slides a cold hand down his honeyed shoulders and long legs and tight buttocks. She cups her hand over his large fine penis, a fluttering wingless bird. So this is what good little girls got these days, if they shaved their legs and brushed their teeth and sprayed under their armpits. Becca cannot remember having been well-groomed enough to win this prize. Ah, she forgot. It is hers by default.

"Out!" says Becca, pushing at John with her foot. "Get out of my bed!"

He rolls over and squints, opening one eye.

"Who said you could sleep here last night?" Becca asks and pulls an old bathrobe off the floor, wrapping it around her. It is freezing. Had Gerry turned off the heat before he left? She listens to the phone ringing but doesn't move.

"Mommy!" Tory comes running in, stops suddenly, staring at John's naked body.

"Get a good look," says Becca. "It'll give you something to

aim for."

"Mommy, please. It's the hospital. They want to know if John's here."

"Oh, Christ! Oh, no!" Becca mutters, handing John the phone, watching the color drain gradually from his face and neck and hands.

"Ulli's very, very bad . . . they want me to come." He rummages for his clothes from a pile on the floor. "They tried calling me at home. Christopher gave them your number," he says, his voice breaking.

Becca looks out the window. We have implicated all the little children, she thinks. John is taking horrible breaths, deep like hiccups, and pouring cognac into a flask.

"Breakfast," he grins crookedly.

Ulli has been moved to the intensive-care unit. There is a special elevator for guests. The nurse at the desk has been given explicit instructions that Becca may not be admitted.

"She must come with me," John says, holding her hand, then dropping it.

The nurse makes a phone call, sighs. "Well, all right, if she behaves herself. No picnics and no screaming." She surveys Becca's overalls and T-shirt, obviously the mourning costume of an unstable person.

They walk down a silent corridor to a room at the end of the hall, the long walk to Hell, thinks Becca. Three nurses stand in a galley of video screens, and recording devices bleep and blink like the pinball machines at the shopping mall. Ulli lies atop a hard bed, white as marble, a *gisant* of a medieval lady asleep on her final slab. Ulli is so thin, and under the sheet she is naked except for tubes and wires and electrodes held with squishy jelly. Her skin is cold, and when Becca touches her thigh, it is grainy, like unglazed clay. She takes Ulli's hand and kneads, trying to warm it. One foot, already purple and cold, sticks out from the bottom of the sheet. When Becca reaches to cover it, her tears drop onto Ulli's solid foot.

"I can't watch this," John says and walks out of the room. Becca holds Ulli's hand, watches her silent face, looks out the one long window in the room. Outside, spring is beginning. Becca, a city child, had never noticed how leaves grow until she had gone to school in Vermont. She had never noticed how they begin tiny, miniatures of themselves, how they unroll and grow and grow every day. How the color changes from pale to dark as the air warms and the days grow longer.

"Oh, Ulli, please don't die, please don't die," prays Becca. "Oh, your hand is so cold, so cold."

Where are the last minute confessions? Becca desires something long and operatic. Ulli will rise from the pillow, long blond hair restored and streaming down the back of a silk gown: "If I die, Becca, I want you to have John," she will sing.

"Oh, Ulli, oh, Ulli, I could not, I could not," goes Becca's aria.

"And I beg of you, Becca, to raise Christopher as your own. My last wish."

But all Ulli can do is move her mouth as if she is chewing some stringy meat; no sounds come out. Ulli is dying a modern death.

"I love you, Ulli," Becca says, alone with her words at last.

A nurse, suddenly considerate, touches Becca on the arm and asks her to leave now.

John is in the waiting room, pouring cognac into a Styrofoam cup of machine coffee. A group of people with Bibles watch him, trying to figure out where they have seen him before. Becca takes a long swig from the flask; the spin is welcome.

Ulli's doctor strides into the room. He puts an arm around Becca and an arm around John and draws them into a tight little triangle, like football players planning their strategy. The doctor whispers. John does not cry; he is not from a weeping background. Becca cries, she stares at the doctor with personal animosity: she will have to grow old without Ulli.

She collects Christopher at school and takes him to the Dairy Queen. Christopher, Ulli's son, the golden boy, the only male in their female constellation. He licks the ice cream around and around.

"Hey, this is neat," he says, cautiously.

"I didn't take you out of school to feed you an ice cream," begins Becca.

"Mama died. Right?" he asks, cold and silken as the soft vanilla ice cream.

"Becca reaches out to take his hand.

"Don't touch me, Becca!" he shouts, like an adult.

Becca dreams of her daughters and Christopher. One daughter is on top, one beneath him; they are locking Christopher in a dangerous sandwich.

Eight

Ulli's mother sends instructions in a two-page telegram, written completely in Swedish. Had she counted on Ulli to translate it?

The entire Scandinavian Language Department gone for the weekend, Becca must wing it. She lifts the heavy volume, Ulli's bluebound *Svensk/Engelsk* dictionary onto her lap. Ulli/Becca, she thinks, running her hand over the cover; another language, another province of the heart. Why hadn't she paid attention to Ulli's Swedish? Another missed educational opportunity. Towards the end, when Ulli often spoke only in Swedish, Becca dreamed her own mouth would open and the Swedish words would float out like balloons in comic strips.

Tiny accent marks sprinkle like coarse salt across her blurry vision. She translates: plans, funeral, occupied, this summer. Becca slams the telegram into the dictionary; Ulli is hers now, her gift, her legacy. She embarks upon tasks and decisions, so bizarre, surrealistic in the land of the living. Having discovered Ulli's trick, she floats outside reality.

Oh, boy, thinks Becca, this is just a bad dream, this is Disneyland, Buñuel. Is the air in this place really moving? It is as hazy as angel's hair in here, and where is the canned religious muzak coming from? Can you get a model with an 8-track cassette? she wonders. Becca prefers to think of them as boats, barges, gondolas; coffins line the walls of the showroom at the funeral home.

"Blue," says Becca. "Definitely blue. Blue is Ulli's color for sure," she says about the quilted lining and satin pillow for the long nap, wrapping her arm through the undertaker's, Mr. MacKenzie. "What do you think, John? Blue?"

John lags behind, his Pilgrim blinders on. "Whatever you think, Becca."

Becca vaguely remembers from Grandpops' funeral that the lids of the coffins must not be bolted down for Jews so the soul may sail out and join the others when the Messiah (finally!) comes. Becca can see Grandpops' tiny soul, flapping its bedsheets, as in a Casper the Friendly Ghost cartoon.

Becca and John select Ulli's coffin. The first piece of furniture for our new life, thinks Becca.

"Becca, I . . . hate . . . to a-a-ask you th-this, but I have to v-view the b-bbbody before they close . . ."

Becca taps a toe impatiently, it may take John months to get this out. "Sure, John," Becca agrees casually. She takes his hand and they walk into an anteroom.

Only the upper half of the Dutch-door lid is open. Her knees parting, Becca stares at Ulli's painted face. It is the Sleeping Beauty who dozed in the window of Madame Tussaud's on Tremont Street the spring that Alexy had taken root in a corner of Becca's womb. Alexy. Alexy sees Death everywhere these days; it hides in her closet, under her bed.

Becca walks closer, looks at the painted face. "It's not Ulli," she says.

"Wha-at?" Mr. MacKenzie falls back, paling.

"Of course, it is," says John, twisting Becca's arm. "Becca, stop it!"

"Better work at Tussaud's. A motor," she informs Mr. MacKenzie evenly.

"Oh," he says, "Yes, yes, of course, certainly. I understand perfectly, Mrs. Solomon." Mackenzie clucks and bows, and as they back out of the room, he nods in relief to an unseen spirit to seal the coffin.

"Becca, come out of there!" There is pounding on the door; Becca hears a jumble of male voices.

"Go away, leave me alone!" She sits in a corner of the ladies' room. There isn't much time left: she will kidnap Ulli, open the lid with the tip of a barrette, lift her out carefully. The makeup may smudge Becca's new black dress, smear her arms, never mind. She will lift Ulli as she did that afternoon in the kitchen. Becca has the strength of a million men now. She will carry Ulli home, prop her up in the rocking chair, cross her silken legs.

"Becca, come out right now!" It is Gerry.

"Becca, please." John's voice.

"Mrs. Solomon, we can't start without you." Ah, it is Mr. MacKenzie, her new beau.

"Come and get me!" she calls.

Becca has played the bathroom game many times; her

favorite childhood retreat, she often hid in the big harlequin-tiled bathroom of her grandparents' apartment. Once, lying in the bathtub, her thumb in her mouth, her hand in her panties, she heard the door open with a click, recognized the small light step all of her grandfather's sons possessed, heard the toilet seat bang against the top, the hiss of zipper teeth, the thick stream that followed. Becca peeked around the shower curtain to see her father: a garden hose, a snake, but red and huge, on fire.

Oh, God. She places her arms around the trunk of the washbasin, presses her hot forehead to it. For just a minute, she would like to join Ulli, lie down on those satin sheets next to her. But she cannot afford that kind of aloneness. "This is the last day of the rest of your life," recites Becca, paraphrasing the words of a poster that hung on her door during the sixties.

"All right, Becca, we're coming in there," Gerry says through the keyhole.

"Give me a minute, I'm coming out," she shouts. She must go, leave her sanctuary. There are three children out there who need her, need her official standing as "Mother." She rinses her face with cold water, swallows a little green-and-yellow pill, prescribed for this very purpose.

There is a fumbling, scraping at the door; the lock turns. Of course, there is a master key, there always is. John and Gerry rush into the room; someone throws on the light switch.

"Okay, I surrender," she says, walking out with her arms raised above her head.

"Becca, please try to behave," begs John.

So many people come. People are scattered around the downstairs of Ulli's house, eating paté sandwiches and drinking the nice muscadet John selected from the wine cellar this morning. They wipe their mouths carefully with the linen cocktail napkins Ulli ironed herself, months ago.

Becca looks around Ulli's living room, filled with the people with whom she has spent most of her adult life, standing hushed like the good children they have always been: Eagle Scouts, valedictorians, prom queens, overachievers all. Only these children at Ulli's funeral are beginning to wrinkle, and go bald and gray, their wombs are empty and sagging, their pricks limp as airless footballs, their major organs slowing to a foxtrot.

She sees the women she marched with and took courses with and taught dance to, and the husbands who called to fix things. She notices her guru, wearing shoes these days and a wraparound skirt with leaping frogs. She answers to "Mary Jean" again. Will the holes in her nose and ears fully close without leaving scars? Becca wonders. There have been a few changes in couples, but it is like the mere rearrangement in the passenger list on the Ark; otherwise, they have all gone forward as predicted.

Groups of people part, step backwards to let Becca pass, dancers in a gavotte. The death of a young woman is an event, an occasion. Cross yourself three times, throw salt over your shoulder. If it happens to someone else, it may not happen to you. Statistics.

Becca looks for her daughters, finds them in the TV room playing Monopoly with Gerry and Angelica. They are silent. Too polite to comment on current events, the girls stare white-faced into the future. Gerry and Angel are being "supportive," Gerry's word; he begins to rise and go to Becca when she comes in. She shakes her head and signals him to sit.

Becca escapes to the back porch, opens the freezer, finds an unopened half-gallon of ice cream, Heavenly Hash, tears off the top and quickly digs her fingers into it, scooping up the cold mush with her hands, hardly swallowing the last bite before she stuffs more in. She shovels diligently, hungrily, ice cream stuck in her nails, numbing the tips of her fingers, dripping down her chin.

"Mommy?"

Becca turns around part way, closing the ice-cream carton, nauseous and embarrassed.

"I didn't know where you were, Mommy."

"I'm sorry. I was putting some things away."

"I couldn't find you," Alexy whines.

"I'm sorry."

"John wants you. He wants you to say goodbye to someone."

"Okay," Becca whispers hoarsely. "I'll be right there."

"Mommy?"

"What?"

"I won't tell."

The next day, Gerry comes and takes all the children out to the farm with him. John locks the doors and closes the drapes; he rolls up the rugs and puts Frank Sinatra on the turntable. They switch from wine to gin, and dance.

Becca has danced with so many men to so many tunes. "Ulli and I danced with Malcolm and Todd to this at the Cape that summer," she tells John and hums between her teeth.

"Who?"

"The guys who lived next door."

"The fairies?"

Becca sighs. "They came for dinner one night."

"Ulli never told me about that."

"It was my idea," Becca covers hastily, forgetting it doesn't matter.

"Ulli didn't tell me many things, Becca. She didn't talk a lot, you know."

Ulli talked to Becca all the time, told her many things.

John goes to the window and slams it shut, as if to keep

Ulli out of the room. Becca tries to teach him the Latin Hustle.

"They thought Ulli and I were lovers," she says slyly to shock him.

John stops dancing, opens his hand and slaps Becca swiftly across the face. She falls down. He has hit her almost exactly in the place where she was cut before, as if he has claimed the territory.

"Did you hit Ulli all the time?" she asks coldly. It stings, but there is no blood.

"No, I didn't hit Ulli." He rubs his head with his hands.

"I must bring out the best in you."

"Oh, Becca," he says and walks across the room in two long strides. He bends down to help her up. "I didn't hit Ulli, I promise."

Becca collapses against John, weeps into his chest, her body slackens against his, but she knows this comfort is temporary.

"I didn't hit Ulli, but I never held her like this, either, Becca. I never saw Ulli cry. Never. When they told her about her tumor, I . . . I wanted to cry! I wanted to scream, to kill!" He takes a deep breath and, letting go of Becca, punches the fireplace mantle. One of the crystal candlesticks flies off, shatters on the floor. "But Ulli just said, 'So. Now I will know how I will die.' "

Becca stares as John stoops over, picking up the shattered glass. She remembers Gerry stepping on the glass at their wedding, the traditional end of the ceremony. It was a fine crystal goblet, one of her grandmother's, wrapped in a thick linen handkerchief. "Nothing but the best for Becca," Grandpops had said.

There is a sharp shard of glass in John's palm. Becca pulls it out, takes his wound into her mouth, sucking out the blood. "Blood brothers," she smiles at John.

Becca knows they will talk all night, will share secrets at

last; there will be a lyrical undressing of the soul, months after that first hectic corporeal one. They will make love on the floor, against the doors to the dining room, settling finally on the roll of rugs in the corner. John will close his eyes; Becca never does.

John says they must collect themselves, stop this, make plans. Becca wants to mourn like her ancient ancestors: rend her clothing, grow a stubble of beard upon her smooth chin, drag orange crates home from the market to squat on, beat her lumpy chest with her clawlike fists. But John's more successful ancestors caution no.

Becca starts to look for Ulli in her own house; Ulli is missing but has left clues and souvenirs everywhere. The rooms are the scene of a dozen parties Ulli gave over the years: dirty ashtrays, smeared wine glasses. Becca searches for Ulli in the photograph albums with the velvet skins and onion pages, through the dried flower arrangements in Nouveau vases, among Christmas decorations and recipes.

In the bedroom are Ulli's favorite pictures of John: John in tails and white tie accepting an award in New York, John the skipper of a yawl in Sweden. John. Ulli's man, now Becca's.

Becca has inherited this from Ulli. She can take down the pictures from Ulli's wall and nail them on her own. Instant family, like the boxes of mashed potatoes at the A & P. For years Ulli prepared Becca for this moment, shared her memories and exercises of the soul with her, passed down her crafts, for this purpose. Becca stands in front of a large chestnut mirror they had both spotted at a rummage sale years ago. They had found it at the same moment, both reached for it: Ulli's smooth tapered fingers, Becca's short bitten ones, had touched for one second, until Becca had taken her hand away. Now it is hers.

She pulls off her dress, her mourning dress, softly

wrinkled and smelling from days of wear. Her underpants, damp and sticky, lie somewhere in the empty fireplace. She showers swiftly using Ulli's soap, sandlewood, steps into Ulli's silky underwear, fastens one of Ulli's French bras. Searching through her fragrant closet, she selects an old dress, white organza, a bridal gown, perhaps, and pulls it over her head. It is big in places, small in others, it doesn't really fit at all. Becca looks into the mirror, sees John standing behind her, his mouth open slightly, his face moist with tears.

"Oh, John, I'm sorry," Becca says and shrugs, runs out of the room, out of the house.

Ulli's black clogs are lined up at the door, as always. Becca steps into them, tears dripping, tracing veins in the leather. So many scenes fly through her head: exits and entrances, the cast of characters varying only in size and ages over all the years: two women, three children. She wishes she could have a large dose of scopolamine, a dream of a drug that leaves one unaware, not only of what happened during an unpleasant event, but for hours before and afterward, too. Becca might erase whole portions of her life this way, set the time dial back to before she knew and needed Ulli. Becca, pre-Ulli, what was she? Who can remember?

She wants to go home, she wants her daughters. She wants to see them, their fat braids and sticky hands and dirty necks. Their familiarity. She needs to hear their thick tangled voices in the middle of the night.

In Ulli's big car, she drives out to the farm. Gerry is chopping wood, barechested. Some hairs are turning gray, she recognizes the beginnings of a bald spot, a silver dollar on his freckled skull. She is going to grow old without him, too, she realizes painfully. She has known this man almost half of her life, and he is no longer hers. She remembers the plaster bride and groom, balanced precariously, on top of their towering wedding cake. For years, a piece of that cake in a white box with her monogram on it sat in the freezer of each house she lived in, moved from place to place diligently. One night, when she was on a diet, she ate it. Gerry does not see her.

The girls are making granola in the kitchen with Angelica. Peeking into a window like a thief, Becca watches them; handfuls of oats and honey stick between their fingers. They suck the fingertips. Alexy sits on a high stool in her nightgown, knees drawn up to her chin, so that Becca sees the faint etching of pubic hair on her oldest daughter. She will have her period soon, thinks Becca.

"I'll never do that," said Alexy once, watching Becca change her Tampax in a French field.

"Oh, yes you will!" Becca promised, bitchily.

She thinks how they plucked out Ulli's womb, scooped it out, "for her convenience," the doctors told Becca. She remembers her mother surreptitiously handing over a packet of brochures about growing up, wrapped in brown paper. She was better at conveying table manners than sexual habits.

"Alexy! Tory!" Becca whispers to the window, but they wouldn't be happy to see her, hear the Mother's voice, always souring, whining, admonishing them, pushing them towards a standard of civilization as outdated as a crinoline slip. What heavies mothers play and always have. Becca's own mother in white gloves and picture hats, lunching at the Walnut Room at Marshall Field's, punctuating mouthfuls of chicken croquettes with admonishments: "Don't point, Rebecca!" "Don't put your elbows on the table!" "Don't talk with your mouth full!"

Oh, Mother, Mother, why did you give up before we could become friends?

My lovely daughters, begins Becca in her head. Lick your fingers, put your whole fucking hands in your mouths.

Look, your father has passed over this paragon of middle-class girlhood for Angelica, who had to lick her fingers and much else on her way up.

She peeks at Angelica's swinging breasts and big grin, her lovely buck teeth. Sisterhood; that notion was supposed to be institutionalized in the sixties. Could Becca do it? Take Angelica aside, be the first wife in the harem, instruct her, guide her to adulthood, be what Ulli had been for her.

Becca waves to her daughters, real sisters who will not touch out of choice for many years. Near the barn, Becca notices a small tortoise-shell cat with two balls of kittens, sucking madly, underneath her, while she sits rigid, at attention, gazing straight ahead.

She drives back to John, who she supposes is slicing his wrists with the French Chef knives by now.

But John stands by the sink, washing wine glasses by hand, dressed in pressed jeans and a clean shirt. "Would you like some breakfast, Becca?"

"John," she whispers.

"Shall I fix you an omelette?"

"John. I'm not Ulli, John."

"Get into bed, Becca, and I'll bring you breakfast," he says harshly.

" 'I have been a stranger in a strange land,' " thinks Becca and laughs, remembering it was the title of the book Gerry was reading on the bus to Selma.

The sun is shining in the bedroom; down comforters in starched covers sit politely folded at the foot of the bed, waiting for Becca. She crawls into them. John brings her fruit and cream, a buttery omelette, thin toast spread with jam, dark coffee with thick cream.

The problem with surviving, thinks Becca in Ulli's bed, is that one must pack up one's guilt like fragile crystal, and carry it in the body, a soft sack, a vessel unsuited for such a long arduous journey.

PART IV

One

"Well," says John, soon, too soon, after. "Shall we live in your house or mine?"

It is almost summer and they are sitting on the porch of Becca's house; the air stinks of insect repellent and burnt hamburgers. Becca wonders if her daughters will remember those as the odors of their childhoods, just as hers smelled of flaky pastry and perfume.

In a corner sits a domed metallic barbecue, new, nasty as a modern sculpture.

"I always wanted one, I could never get that brick thing going," John confessed to Becca the afternoon he brought it over and put it together. Now he is lying next to it on a chaise, swatting mosquitos with a long-handled spatula, dressed in an apron that accompanied the grill. DAD IS THE CHEF announce a hundred dancing hot dogs with puffy hats and big grins.

"My house has slightly higher property values, but yours is closer to the school. It may be more easily expandable, too. . . ."

"Are you asking me to marry you?"

"Well, h'm, yes'm," John slurs, blushing slightly. "I mean since we already . . ."

"You mean since we're already fucking?" Becca says.

"Becca," he sighs. The children sit like a cautious jury across from them on the picnic bench.

Becca knows she should feel grateful, that she has won a kind of prize. Is this how mothers feel who have the most beautiful baby in the nursery? Becca has won John, this beauty, this stud, this champion media macho man. But how? Simply by default; she and John are the consolation prize.

He pours them both more wine, outlining plans to the children, who are jumping excitedly around him. "We'll all take a long honeymoon to the Islands, rent a house on St. Croix. . . ."

Becca isn't really listening; something is wrong, something is missing. Becca needs the wooing. And where is the element of surprise? There is something too tidy about this, it smacks of Old Testament convenience.

"Do you love me?" Becca asks.

"Oh," says John, as if he has forgotten to read aloud the American League scores. "Sure."

"Sure?" Becca smiles at him weakly. "Sure?"

Oh, Mac, thinks Becca, you were not right about me. Having led a terrestrial life, I need to climb mountains, strange mountains, closed at one time to foreigners, but open lately to women of taste and talent. I will shortly embark on a dangerous voyage. Alone.

"No, John," says Becca, "I won't marry you."

"Mommy!" Tory shouts and runs over, slaps her hand over Becca's mouth.

"What's the matter?" Becca tastes salt on her daughter's hand.

"Oh, Mommy, please."

"Hey!" says Becca. "This isn't the Brady Bunch or something. It doesn't call for a group decision."

"But I like John," Alexy whispers to Becca.

"I like John, too," says Becca. "I just don't want to marry him."

"Well, I do," says Tory. "He wasn't just asking you, you know, he was asking all of us to marry Christoph and him."

John is twirling the ketsup bottle between his hands, a pirouetting dancer, and looking at the used paper cups. And Christopher; he is withdrawing so quickly these days, Becca must rush over to touch him, put an arm around him. Their shoulders meet: equals.

"Hey, Christoph," Becca says, "I love you. You know that. I just can't be Ulli. You understand that, don't you?"

He shrugs. Becca knows that shrugging will be his chief gesture for many years. And John, he is so hurt, too, stinging from the loss of Ulli.

"Oh, John," she says and takes his hand, puts the palm flat against her warm face, kisses it. Dear John, her first man-friend. She, too, needs every connection with Ulli, but not like this. "It wouldn't work," she whispers, full of tears.

"But it would, Becca. That's the point, it would be so easy."

"Why? Because we have all the equipment? Do you think we can just go to the store and outfit our lives like Ken and Barbie? That isn't what I want!"

"You don't know what you want," he mumbles.

"Oh, no, you're wrong. I do know what I want, or at least I know what I don't want." Becca wants to dance, dance over these bodies, over the rooftops of this little town, over this life. "I don't want to play house, John. I want to live my life, not imitate Ulli's."

Becca dreams she is teaching Ulli how to drive a car. In reality, of course, it would have been ridiculous. Becca is a spotty, erratic, imaginative driver; Ulli could have hauled an open truck of eggs down a busy highway without cracking one. She never allowed Becca to drive her anywhere, until she was sick.

But, in the dream, Becca is teaching Ulli, only Ulli is a large life-size rubber mannequin, the kind used in teaching hospitals, like busty Betty or whatever her name is, whose lumpy breasts sit on a shelf in Becca's doctor's office, waiting for hundreds of searching fingers.

"This is an exact replica," promises the man from whom Becca purchases Ulli.

Becca slings her over her shoulder. Ulli is naked, but lacking sexual organs, like Becca's first rag doll. Becca props her up, in the driver's seat, placing her hands on the steering wheel. The only problem is that Ulli keeps flopping over, first her head, then her arms drop down, one by one, and Becca must keep replacing her hands on the wheel, holding them there, steering the car herself.

They are driving down the squiggly, checkered road of the Game of Life, in their pink plastic convertible. But the sun is so hot Ulli is beginning to melt and drip, sliding down the car seat, dissolving into a puddle on the floor of the car.

"John!" Becca screams, waking. "Gerry," she tries more softly. But John did not spend the night, he barely said goodbye, and Gerry is long gone.

Becca takes a trip, Becca alone, one suitcase in the back seat of a compact car, rented, belonging to no one. She is heady with freedom, does not agree with Janis Joplin, that "Freedom's just another word for nothin' left to lose." Becca is not a victim of the sixties, after all, she is a survivor. Maybe people have decades that suit them, Grandpops on a twenties stage, her aunties stuck in the forties, her parents forever fifties, Gerry groping out of the sixties. Becca will be the woman of the future.

Oh, Ulli, you have given me this spirit, this breath, this new life. Where has Becca learned about this transmigration of the soul?

Life is supposed to be a journey, birth and death the major stops. The soul takes a trip, a boat trip, Becca recalls. Was it the ancient Greeks who placed a silver coin in the mouth of the deceased so she could pay Charon for the trip across the River Styx to the Elysian fields? Ulli lives in Heaven, a space Becca has furnished basically in Bauhaus with a few good antiques, like Ulli's living room.

Becca steers her car down the winding ribbon to the Cape. For her first stop, she selects a Holiday Inn in one of the ugliest cities in America. This is my first adventure, my first solo flight, my maiden voyage, she wishes to inform the desk clerk, as she signs the register, but, of course, she does not.

Becca notices right away that children under twelve may stay free in your room and eat without charge in the plastic dining room, and she feels empty.

"My children are at home," she explains. With their father and his lover, she does not add, part of the new extended family. "I shall bring them next time, for sure," she reassures the desk clerk. "No, just one suitcase, I can carry it myself."

"This is my first real adventure," she says to herself in the mirror and writes Tory and Alexy a postcard.

Becca puts on her new bathing suit and takes the elevator down to the pool. She takes a seat on a contour lounge chair and opens her book. All around her, other people's children are engaging in dangerous water acts: two toddlers waddling out of the shallow end, a bunch of boys diving on the heads of other boys. But Becca is no longer the lifeguard at this pool; her term of duty is about over. Once, at another Holiday Inn, a little old lady in Sunday dress snapped Becca and Gerry and Tory and Alexy tossing a bright orange ball in a circle in a pool: The American Family.

She goes back upstairs and calls her daughters at the farm. "Tory?"

"Who is this?"

"It's me, Mommy."

"Oh. What do you want?"

"I just wanted to talk to you, Tor."

"Oh. Well, I'm busy. Goodbye."

"Don't hang up!" Becca screams. "May I speak to Alexy?"

"She doesn't want to talk to you."

"Why not?" But Becca is sure she is right.

"She's on a horse. Ha, ha. Wa-it, Daddy wants to talk to you."

"No . . . wait, Tory, no . . ." She hears the receiver drop, hears Gerry sigh.

"Becca, what's the matter?"

"Nothing's the matter. I just wanted to say hello to my children. I'm very involved with their well-being."

"You saw them this morning."

"I just wanted to tell them I'm fine."

"Are you at the Cape already?"

"No, I thought I'd drive slowly, enjoy it all. I'm having a wonderful time," she laughs gaily. "I'll call tomorrow."

What Becca would really like is a drink. She would like to go down to the bar, but she is afraid; downstairs, she fears, will be lurking traveling salesmen, the heroes of a dozen of Grandpops' jokes. She dials the lobby. "Room service, please."

"Room service? There's no room service, lady."

No room service. Becca has been left to inhabit a world without amenities. She makes her way to the bar. It is damp and formica, but it is empty. She orders a gin and tonic and wishes for one minute the bartender would bring a Shirley Temple, a youthful concoction of grenadine and ginger ale, with a paper parasol piercing a maraschino cherry.

"Would the young lady like a Shirley Temple?" a cocktail waitress once asked Grandpops.

"Thank you very much," said Grandpops, who thought she said Becca looked just like Shirley Temple.

Becca stares at her face in the long bar mirror. No mistaking Becca for Shirley Temple any longer.

"At some point, my darling," Aunt Fanny once confided sadly, "you will have to decide if you wish to be seen coming or going."

Becca did not understand.

"From the front or from the back, darling. If the bummy is too skinny, the face may be scrawny. And vicie versie, Becca."

She must decide if she is coming or going.

Becca calls her parents in Florida. The phone rings three times before she hears: "This is Joey Schuman. Judy and I are not home now. We are out playing golf or tennis, enjoying our new life style. If you would like us to call you back, just leave a message. You have sixty seconds after you hear the 'beep.' So long!"

Becca is absolutely stunned; she manages only to get out "cha-cha-cha" before she is cut off.

It is Ulli she would like to call, would like to hear from. Becca remembers her first taste of death. One of the aunties, Estelle, succumbed to female disorders when Becca was ten. They did not tell Becca for a whole day, Grandpops in favor of passing the whole thing off as a family reunion. But her parents insisted that she be told, afraid that she would break into song and dance at inappropriate moments.

It was left to Grandma Rosie, a makeupless ghost herself, to tell Becca. "Oh, Beccala," crooned Grandma Rosie, rocking her in silken arms. "Just pretend Auntie has gone on a long trip. Remember when she went to California and was gone all summer?"

"Yes," sniffled Becca, "but then she sent me post cards."

How had Grandma Rosie arranged for those post cards? Those matted, color-smeared scenes of the West: purple sunsets, red-costumed Children of Chinatown, the Temple of Aimee Semple McPherson, Opening Night at the Hollywood Bowl.

Becca understood the game well enough not to study postmarks or compare handwritings. Oh, write me a letter, Ulli, send me a card, thinks Becca, falling asleep. I will not check.

In August, Becca sits in the lobby of a New York hotel, waiting to meet Ulli's mother. She has resisted this moment for days, since the mother called. Her voice, her phrasing, all this is too familiar, Becca knows, for her own good. But she has popped a couple of friendly pills and changed her clothes several times, trying to create a proper image from some shirts and scarves and shoes, and sits on a flat leather banquette, waiting for Ulli to walk out of the elevator.

Becca recognizes Ulli's mother immediately, but not because of a striking resemblance. There are some similarities, but where Ulli was angular and always tanned, the mother is softer, rounder, with wonderful skin, the kind of pink and white achieved by hours and hours of facials and skin care and moisturizers, Becca suspects. She is older than Becca imagined she would be, a woman narrowing at the bottom and thickening at the top, neat, fashionably dressed. She offers a gloved hand, like the Queen.

"Ah, so this is Becca," she smiles.

Becca, no stranger to form, almost curtsies. "Yes. . . ."

"But you must call me Katya," she smiles again. "I hate it when these young women and men call me 'Aunt' or 'Countess'. . . ."

"Katya," practices Becca who has no intention of calling Ulli's mother "Aunt" or "Countess."

"It is all right to eat in the hotel, or perhaps you would prefer some place else?"

"No, no, this is lovely." It has been years since she has eaten in a restaurant like this, with thick starched cloths on the round tables, ice water in goblets, one rose bending in a tarnished holder. She follows Ulli's mother to the table the way she would have her mother or Grandma Rosie or one of the aunties.

"Will you have something to drink?" asks the mother.

"I'd love a glass of wine, please."

"Ah, good. I, also. Shall we drink a bottle?" she asks, conspiratorially. "It will loosen up the tongue, perhaps," she smiles.

Becca's problem is keeping her mouth shut; she hopes she will succeed.

"You are much different than I thought," says Ulli's mother.

"Oh?"

"*Jo*. Ulli sent me a picture of you both. I think it is rather old, from Cape Cod. . . ." She opens a huge Italian bag and piles matching-leather address books, makeup cases, a pair of enormous sunglasses on the pink tablecloth. "Here it is. . . ." She pulls out a photocase, flips through it, extends a picture.

Becca and Ulli sit at the wooden table on the porch, glasses raised in celebration. Ulli wears a flowered sundress, Becca hides in John's hat and a pair of cutoffs and her "God" T-shirt. Ulli had set the automatic timer and rushed, laughing, from behind the tripod so she and Becca could capture themselves for all time.

"Well," Becca manages to say, finally, "that was years ago. My hippie stage."

"Hmmm," Katya says. "Ah, good, the wine. *Skoal*, Becca!"

L'chaim, thinks Becca and remembers to sip.

"You must think I am very bad not to come when Ulli is sick and when she dies," says the mother.

Whew! That was fast, thinks Becca, holding onto the table. This woman is really expert at playing Truth.

"But . . . she did not want me to come. She wrote me, no."

Becca stares at her omelette, sprouting globules of butter. She puts down her fork.

"I saw so little of her all those years of her growing up. I had to escape from my own life and I let Ulli escape, too. You must understand." She is back into her purse. "Cigarette?"

"Please."

"When I left Sweden for Paris after the war, it was my way of breaking from my husband's family. His mother was a terrible, frightening woman, very powerful. Sweden is a very rigid society. People think we are free-living, but it is full of rules and regulations for people in our position."

Becca thinks of Sven. Passion is black, Sven had said to Becca. She would like to touch him, just tap his shoulder for one minute right now.

"And when I give up Ulli to the Sisters of the *Sacre Cœur*, it was my way of making her free of me, of Sweden. Do you understand that just a little?"

"Ulli was a very happy person," says Becca.

"Ah, Becca, do you think so, really?" the mother asks, and in that breath, that space, the pause Ulli always took at the beginning of a sentence, Becca hears her voice.

"Oh, yes, she was really happy with her life. Satisfied. She wasn't even angry about dying. I was really impatient with her, but she laughed at me. 'Ah, Becca, I cannot complain. I have done many nice things.' "

"I should like to think so. There is so much guilt, Becca, from the beginning, guilt from her father . . . Ah, I was so young and the times were so strange."

"Do you know about Lars?" asks Becca, not really curious, not wanting to be cruel, but feeling she has been left as Ulli's advocate on this earth.

The mother breathes deeply and raises her hand to her throat. "Lars. What he . . . did to her?"

"Yes."

"Ah, Becca, it is so hard for me to admit this to someone. For years I did not know what happened. Then, one day, Lars comes to me and tells me when Ulli was fourteen she forced him to make love to her . . . and I, I do not think." The mother is crying. She shuffles through the bag for a handkerchief and puts on her sunglasses.

"The last thing Ulli said, that I heard her say," Becca tells her mother, "was . . . oh God, I know I'm not going to pronounce it properly . . . 'Mama, vill du gå med på badstrand?' "

"Mama, will you go with me to the beach?" the mother whispers. "Thank you, Becca."

"So. Becca," Ulli's mother says as they swivel through the front doors into the sunlight. She puts her arm through Becca's and pats her hand. "I should like to have Christopher come and stay for a while with me. What do you think? Will he like that?"

"Ask Christoph. Ask John," says Becca. They pass a series of vendors; Becca feels suddenly hungry.

"You are his guardian, I understand."

"But only if something happens to John," Becca explains. "I'd like to think of myself as his fairy godmother."

Ulli had appointed Becca Christopher's guardian and

one of the executors of her will. Becca had been amazed, thrilled by Ulli's faith in her. Becca feels her pull continuously, as if Ulli possesses the long finger of Michelangelo's God on the Sistine Chapel ceiling.

"I should like a chance with Christopher," the mother says wistfully. "I wish John would not move to California. It is so far from Sweden."

It is so far from Becca. John has slipped back behind his makeup mask, reverted to his public voice when he has to communicate with Becca at all; he has taken a job as the host of a morning talk show in L.A.

"So. Shall we go on to the museum?"

"What museum?"

"I did not mention it to you over the phone, Becca? There is an Avedon exhibit at the Metropolitan?"

"No," sighs Becca, not ready for this, but she leaves her arm in the mother's.

"What will you do, Becca? With your life?"

"With my life?" repeats Becca. "Well, for starters, I'm being divorced."

The mother clucks her tongue. Sympathetically?

"I'm not sure. I've been investigating a dance therapy program in New York. You work with mentally disturbed people, try to bring them out with dance movement." Becca sighs. "I don't even know if I could do that, but dancing is the only thing I know about."

"You could not just be a dancer?"

"Oh, no, I'm much too old and I've been away from it for too long. The life of the dancer is very brief," explains Becca. "Very beautiful and very brief."

There are three photographs of Ulli in the first room of the exhibit; small square pictures that had originally appeared in *Vogue*: Ulli in famous French clothes in Paris. In the first, she wears a little collared coat, playing pinball with a smooth young man; in another, Ulli leans over a cafe table, the hooped skirt of her dress lifting slightly, like the end of a jacked-up car; in the final shot, she holds up one gloved hand in imitation of a traffic policeman.

"She looks happy," her mother says.

They are not really Ulli, either, Becca thinks in relief. They sit on a bench in front of the photographs.

"You must come to Sweden someday, Becca."

"Perhaps," Becca shrugs.

Two

Becca hops over some packing crates to answer the door on Halloween night. It is too late to be a costumed child; she can see the shadow of a man's shoulder.

"Who is it?" she whispers, nervously. Becca is afraid of so many things lately, the dark being one of them. She sleeps with a light on in her bedroom; Ulli's purple foot floats across the ceiling as in a Chagall. Moving closer to the window, she sees it is Gerry.

"Trick or treat?" asks Gerry, crookedly.

"Oh, let me guess which," sighs Becca. His presence still unnerves her.

"May I come in?"

"Of course, it's your house, in case you've forgotten."

Some settlement; division of a lifetime. Not really interested in the proceedings, victim of legal jargon and feminist leanings, Becca managed to rescue her daughters and a few objects. "Would you like some coffee?" she asks politely.

"Yes, thanks." Gerry walks around the room, picking up familiar things, putting them down in different places. "Still determined to leave town, I see."

"Gerry, we've been through this a million times. I can't keep commuting to my classes, and I have a job all lined up there."

"Hm." He inspects a silver cigarette box that had been Ulli's. "Nice stuff. Still seeing the shrink?"

"You're not paying for it," she snaps. She feels he really should: workman's compensation.

"You were acting pretty crazy, Becca."

She hears the kettle whistling in the kitchen. "Crazy!" she shouts as she retreats. "I'm being divorced, I just watched my closest friend die, and he thinks I'm acting crazy. It turns out I was the original cream-filled ego to begin with, Gerry."

"I could have told you that." He picks up a riding crop off the coffee table, smooths it across his palm. "You into S & M these days?"

Becca remembers Emmett, shudders. "It's Angelica's, by the way. Tory borrowed it for her sheik costume. Alexy was an angel. Cream?"

"No, I'm drinking it black," he says, patting his stomach. "I've got to take off a few pounds."

"It gets harder every year," says Becca. God, she thinks, we sound like ex-roommates at a reunion.

"Wasn't Alexy an angel before?"

"No, that was Tory. Alexy was the devil. I went as God. Don't you remember?"

"Sure," he shrugs. "Alexy's very upset about Ulli."

"I know. We talk about it all the time. Tory told us that

death is only the sixth thing Americans fear the most."

"Where did she get that?"

"Some book of lists or something. Number six."

"What's first?"

"Speaking before a group," Becca smiles.

"Come on."

"Really, ask Tory. Maybe she'll lend you her book. Americans are afraid of all kinds of things first: bugs, heights, bad breath . . ." Becca draws her breath. "You should know that, Gerry, isn't that your field?"

Gerry no longer answers that "sociology is the study of the history, development, organization and problems of people living together in social groups." "Good coffee," he says instead.

"Thank you. I do make good coffee."

"Wow, have you changed! A year ago, you would have denied it or said they were new beans."

"I've gained some confidence. I think John did that for me."

"Tory told me John wanted to marry you." Gerry stares at her over his mug.

Becca sends a silent thank you to her sleeping daughter. "Going to bed with such a stud gave me a higher opinion of my abilities," Becca says and blushes slightly; she has never been this frank with Gerry before.

"I'm surprised you didn't marry him. I always thought you had a crush on John."

"I can't marry John. You know that, Gerry. The second Mrs. de Winter," she mutters under her breath.

"Well, you're certainly making a comeback, Becca."

"A comeback? Oh, like Grandpops at the Old Men's Home."

Gerry follows her into the kitchen, picks at some chicken from a casserole on the stove. "Hmm, good. Is that the one with shallots and cheese?"

"No, it's a new recipe. Mushrooms, prosciutto, a little dry Marsala."

"I wish Angelica would learn how to cook. Do you know what I had for dinner tonight? Baked beans and American cheese."

"Maybe, you'd like it if I came out to the farm and gave her a few lessons?"

"Oh, Becca, would you?"

"Gerry, you're hopeless," she sighs, answering the ringing telephone. "Excuse me . . . hello?"

Gerry walks around the living room, picks up the Tiffany vase, reads the titles of some new books.

"Hi. Yes, of course, I remembered," Becca says into the phone. "See you tomorrow. About eight."

"Is that a man?" asks Gerry.

"Yes," says Becca, amused.

"Someone I know?"

"Uh-huh."

"Don't play games with me, Becca."

"I'm not playing games. It's really none of your business."

"Isn't that my copy of Freud's *Interpretation of Dreams*?"

"Take it."

"Is it someone at the University?"

"Used to be. But you didn't know him well. He has admired me from afar for years, it turns out. Did you know I had admirers for years?"

"Oh, Becca," Gerry says suddenly and throws his arms around her waist, pulling her onto the sofa. "I love you, Becca."

"Gerry, stop this!" Becca tries to pull free of him.

"No, really, Becca, I love you, I love you." He tries to hold her still, kissing her on the mouth.

"This is crazy. Get off me!" Becca sinks her teeth into his shoulder.

"Aw, shit! Goddamn, Becca." He moves away, rubbing

his wound.

"Just stay away from me, Gerry."

"Angelica's pregnant," he says triumphantly.

Becca whistles through her teeth. "You're really planting your garden all over town."

"You're still bitter," he says.

"Me, bitter? No, I'm just tart," she smiles. Shmuck! Why does this bother her so much? Was Becca the keeper of the seed? "Well, I hope you have enough time to get married. The University might not approve."

"We've just been waiting for the divorce to become final. You know that."

"I know that," she agrees. "You really make a habit of it, don't you?"

"What?"

"Knocking up women."

"No one uses that expression anymore, Becca."

"Oh."

"I'd forgotten about . . . you." He smiles tentatively.

"I haven't."

"Oh, Becca, I don't really want to marry Angelica. I want to be married to you. Angel's a stranger."

Some stranger! she thinks, but answers seriously. "Everybody's a stranger. You didn't know me on the bus to Selma."

Gerry takes Becca's hand. She doesn't pull it away. "But I know you now, Becca."

"You don't know me, Gerry. You've just known me longer. You know more facts about me. Facts are snappy, run Angelica through a computer."

"My mother keeps asking for you. Every time we visit, she takes me aside and asks, 'Where's Becca?' "

"Good question," she sighs. "She called me last week. She kept whispering over the phone, as if she were a conspirator."

"I told her she could see you."

"I know." Becca starts to laugh. "Oh, God, that reminds me of something."

"What's so funny?"

"I just remembered the advice my father gave me before we were married. We were standing at the top of the aisle and he said . . ."

"Don't, Becca! It makes me sad."

"Daddy!" Tory was standing on the stairs in her night-gown, the mustache from her costume hanging on an angle.

"Hi, Tor."

"What are you doing up?" asks Becca.

"I just wanted to make sure you weren't eating all my trick-or-treat candy."

"Thanks a lot. I haven't touched it."

Tory signals to Becca, pointing her finger towards the kitchen. "Come here," she whispers. "Is Daddy coming home?"

"Oh, Tory, what makes you think that?" Becca strokes her daughter's unkempt hair.

"He's here, isn't he?"

"He isn't here," Becca explains. "He's just visiting the scene of the crime."

"I grew up in Chinese restaurants," says Becca.

"That funny. You no lookee Chinese," says Chuck, opening his menu.

Oh God, what a winner! Ethnic jokes, no less! Becca is learning there is a whole new set of rules governing dating these days; there are gaps, spaces, one makes breathtaking leaps. And nothing is forever after, of course.

"What I mean is, we ate Chinese food every Sunday," she sighs. Unable to speak easily to these strange men, she finds herself serving up bits of her childhood.

"Why don't you order for us then, Becca?" he smiles.

Becca orders a banquet from her youth, when China consisted of only two provinces, Peking and Canton. "Sub-gum with won ton, fried rice, shrimp egg foo yong, Chicago chop suey . . ."

"Chicago chop suey?"

"My favorite," she says. "From exactly how afar did you admire me?" asks Becca.

"Well. Once, we sat next to each other at a party," he says. "At your friend's, the Swedish woman who died . . . ?"

"Ulli?" Becca sits up, her palms tingling. "You knew Ulli?"

"Not awfully well. My wife . . . ex-wife took a Chinese cooking course with her, I think."

"Was that the party she made all those spring rolls for? Did we eat Chinese there? Do you remember?"

He shakes his head. "I remembered you."

"Everything Ulli did was so special, so beautiful. She was so beautiful."

"I don't remember that particularly. I thought she was rather big-boned."

"Oh, Ulli was perfect looking, Ulli was gorgeous!" says Becca indignantly.

"You're much more beautiful than Ulli, Becca. Don't you know that?"

Becca looks down at some rice on her lap. "When I was a little girl, I brought the leftovers home in a white paper box and ate them for breakfast Monday morning."

"Will we eat Chinese food for breakfast?" he asks, grabbing her hand.

Luckily, she only needs one hand to eat with chopsticks. Becca tells him about Grandpops, about the cookies he would buy for her, three of them in a rice paper bag, and about the fat wrinkled litchi nuts, like her aunties' faces, shrinking back from their shells, and about the magic clams that, when submerged in the bathroom sink, opened their tight thighs and produced red and blue paper flowers.

"My Grandpops said the Chinese are the only people who are smarter and more ancient than the Jews. That's why we ate so much Chinese food," Becca confides. "What does your fortune cookie say?"

"It says, 'Grab Chinese-Jewish cookie across the table.' "

Becca clears her throat. "Mine says, 'At some age, it is easier to bare the soul than the breast.' "

"Ha, ha," he laughs. "Your place or mine?" he pretends to read from another cookie.

Sliding into his car, Becca says, "My Grandpops sold Cadillacs."

"Oh, fuck your family," he says in a friendly manner, slamming her door.

"Do you have any money?" she asks as they walk out of their apartment building.

"I don't need any money," says Tory.

"Of course, you do," Becca begins to lecture. "This is a big city, this isn't like being in . . ."

"We're just going down the street to school."

"Well, take a dime in case you have to call me."

"You don't need a dime. All you do is dial '0' and call collect."

"Okay," says Becca suddenly. "Forget it. Have a nice day. See you later."

The girls stand and stare. "Mommy!" Alexy shouts after her.

Becca turns around. "What's wrong? I'm going to be late for work."

"I don't know," says Alexy. "You usually ask more questions."

"Like do you have your homework and your gym clothes and a sharp pencil?" Becca asks, amused.

"Yeah," says Tory.

"Well, I don't have time for that anymore. You're big girls. And so am I." She kisses them again and walks off towards the subway.

Becca flies through the heavy door of the clinic where she works. "Am I late?"

"No, Becca, you're fine," says the secretary.

She unlocks the door to the dance therapy room, turns up the lights, raises the rattan shades. Someone's grateful parents had donated it several years ago and unfortunately ordered it furnished as a poshy ballet studio. By the time Becca is working here, the mirrors have all been broken and only dingy little plastic hinges decorate the walls; the posters of Makarova as Giselle are ripped and peeling back from the tape. Only the smooth wood *barre*, unused, survives intact.

Becca grabs it, slips off her clogs, slides her feet into first position. She and Alexy are taking a ballet class on Thursday nights. Becca stands behind her daughter, choking back tears Alexy must not see. In the precarious balance of the world of mothers and daughters, Alexy would drop it in a minute if she knew the intensity of Becca's connection. So Becca watches the soft hollow of her neck, a few random curls, the arch of her thin shoulders, feels she is initiating her daughter into an ancient order.

She wouldn't mind having the mirrors back, she thinks. Must talk to them about that. The confrontation with self isn't a bad idea now and then. Becca starts to sort records for today's session as her group shuffles in.

Their sudden appearance always startles her. They are all women, in late adolescence and their early twenties, all victims of growing up. Several of them have been raped; one, by a gang of five, a high-school basketball team; incest has carried away another. One has responded by gaining almost two hundred pounds; the girl raped by her uncle one weekend suffers from anorexia. It is too painful for her to sit on the floor, the bones at her thighs protrude like the handles of daggers. Becca drags a thick mat over for her.

Watching them assemble, she remembers a poem she wrote for Mac's class, not far from this building, comparing madness to a warm dune, the curve of a mother's breast, something comforting. Now she knows there is no warmth, no comfort, it is a series of nonstop nightmares that never recede. Becca is dancing the daily nightmares of her patients, her sad little corps de ballet.

She greets them very physically, patting arms and shoulders, hugging the ones that hang reluctantly around the door, encouraging someone to put out her cigarette. Then she removes her heavy shirt and skirt, hoping that undressing in front of them will allow them to emulate her freedom. When she started working here, some of the girls would not remove their shoes and socks to dance. Now they all do.

Becca's outfits always elicit a response. Some days she dances in jeans and a T-shirt; other days, dresses as a proper ballerina in pink tights, her hair wound into a tight bun. Today, she is wearing new red leotards.

"Oo la! la! Becca. Red!" Celeste, who is huge but imagines herself a slim temptress, slinks up, passes her hand over Becca's arm.

"Like them? I can get you a pair, Celeste, if you'd like to dance in leotards," says Becca, interested. Celeste presently resides in a denim tent.

"Oh, sure, then she'd look like a barn door," says Nancy, a former beauty queen, who flipped out after her third abortion.

"I would not," whines Celeste and sticks her thumb in her mouth.

"Moo, moo," calls someone from a corner of the room, and they all start walking around Celeste, mooing.

"All right," says Becca, picking up on that. "Let's all be animals, okay?"

She moves towards the records, doing a few bends. They usually begin with warm-up exercises, but she knows Celeste is giving her clues, hidden directions, that must be acted upon. She shuffles quickly through the stack of records, finding some children's albums she used to play for Alexy and Tory and Christopher.

"Let's make a big circle," says Becca and takes Celeste's hand first; it is cool and surprisingly slender. Several of the women fight for Becca's free hand, like children at nursery school. She takes Karen's, promises Lisa for next time. They skip around singing "The Farmer in the Dell," then "Old MacDonald."

The record switches to Woody Guthrie, his children's songs, "Riding in My Car."

Her car loaded with groceries and little children, Becca sang this through the sixties and early seventies, considered Woody Guthrie proper music for future radicals.

Singing, Becca leads the way, starting her engine, and soon her patients are driving around the studio in their pretend cars, revving up their motors, tooting their horns. Becca always hopes for a quick response like this; if she is lucky, something hidden and painful will be uncovered, exposed.

Suddenly, Celeste rushes around the room, breathing heavily, and bumps full force into Becca, knocking her off her feet and crashing her against the *barre*. Becca sinks dizzily to the floor.

Becca is angry, then hurt, blinks back tears, tries to lift herself, looking for Celeste.

"Oh, you bitch, Celeste!" screams Nancy. "You hurt Becca."

"You cow," spits Lisa.

Oh, no, more cow music, thinks Becca wearily, feels for a

huge lump on her head. Celeste crawls over to her, a mass of sobbing, heaving flesh.

"Oh, Becca, I didn't mean to . . . I saw that car and all those boys . . . they were on top of me and . . ."

"Shh, Celeste, it's okay," says Becca putting her arms around this big baby, who smells of her latest meal. "Shh, it's okay."

Woody Guthrie is still singing, obliviously, from the corner of the studio, his sappy, twangy voice, a voice from the past, his song, "So Long."

Becca closes her eyes and sees Ulli climbing on the train to New York. They used to take turns watching the children and going shopping in the city.

At last, Becca has her own magic act; she can conjure up the past at will, recall any image, any time.

Becca and Alexy and Tory and Christopher have driven Ulli to the station. They stand on the platform, barefoot, holding hands, strung across the horizon like a chain of paperdolls, singing, and Ulli is in the window of the train, waving goodbye.

Thoughts on
ADULT EDUCATION
many years later

In the spring, exactly twenty years ago, two women named Becca and Ulli came to live with me. I had recently started working with the poet and novelist Maxine Kumin, who was teaching in the Creative Writing Department at Princeton University for the semester. I had sent her two very short stories — I couldn't write more than five or six pages at that time — and a letter saying: "I am a housewife trying to crawl out of her kitchen." Although I had wanted to be a writer most of my life, it was only six months before that I had begun writing with a certain seriousness I had never brought to my work before, meaning I was actually writing, instead of just talking about it.

We were living on the lake then, in a split-level contemporary house, and the spare bedroom, which had previously housed a series of students who baby-sat in exchange for the room and an occasional meal — other people's difficult adolescent children was how I thought of them — was empty because my children, now 11 and 10, could finally stay home alone. I resigned from all my volunteer activities and gave myself five years to produce one publishable work — a short story, perhaps, in an obscure literary magazine.

I had known Becca a long time, although I didn't know her name. For several years I wanted to write about this woman and the times she lived in; sometimes I called her Susan, sometimes I called her Sandra, but I could never get beyond a few flat first-person narrated pages. One of the stories I had sent Maxine was about a dancer named Becca. All of a sudden I knew the name of this woman! I knew she had been a dancer; I knew she had red hair. I began to see her. More importantly, I heard her voice — she talked to me all the time. The kitchen, my car, my bedroom became cluttered with scraps of paper with what Becca had to say to me. In fact, suddenly, everything anyone told me seemed to be about Becca. Her friend Ulli arrived differently. I had spent the academic year 1973-4 in Sweden, and Ulli became the culmination of that strange, mysterious, beautiful place for me.

I would meet with Maxine in her office every Monday for an hour. She would read what I brought her and I would watch her elegant face for signs of amusement, confusion, pleasure. She taught me that my stories were really outlines and needed to be filled out with details and dialogue. Sometimes she said they were finished as they were, sometimes she didn't have a clue about what to do to save them. After that hour, I would jog indoors in the enormous skeletal university gymnasium — like Jonah in the belly of the whale, I thought — on a wonderful spongy track, and pieces of fiction would float through my head. With my flushed face and all my pulses beating, it was like being in love.

By May, I had written about forty pages about Becca and Ulli and their husbands Gerry and John and the children, Christopher and Alexandra and Victoria. "Well," said Max at our last session together, "if you can write eighty more pages about these four characters, you will have a novella and maybe we can fix up some of these short stories and you will have a book." (A book!) More importantly, Max handed me on to Joyce Carol Oates for a tutorial the next fall.

"No," said Joyce, when I brought her my 75 pages. It's not a novella, it's a short novel — about 180 pages — and here is how you begin."

Each Monday at three o'clock, I climbed the stairs to Joyce's office, usually stopping to chat with Richard Ford across the hall. He had published only one critically acclaimed novel at that point, so I wasn't too intimidated by him, and anyway, he had those lovely Southern manners. I assume he still has. Every week, I brought Joyce the next chapter I had written on the basis of her wise and gentle guidance. One week, I remember I was very distracted and didn't get much done and when Joyce questioned me, I said I was thinking about Thanksgiving and making a turkey. "Well, think about Becca making a turkey," she said.

By April, I had written 180 pages. I remember how Joyce put the manuscript down on her desk and said very seriously, "You are now at a blessed point for any writer. You have a fine first draft of your novel. Treat it as if you will die and this is the only thing that you will leave behind. This is a record of your soul in the year 1979." I started to quibble — not unlike Becca — and say it was the record of my soul for my entire life but then Joyce said that she and her husband would like to bring it out as the first novel of their new publishing company, The Ontario Review Press.

The publication of *Adult Education* in the late spring of 1981 soon took on a Cinderella-like quality: rave reviews, a large trade paperback sale, the sale of foreign rights, a book club sale and an option on the screen rights: rare things for a small press' first novel. Shortly before the Italian edition appeared, a popular Italian magazine sent a journalist and a photographer to interview me. "How had my life changed?" they wanted to know. "Well, you're in my living room," was about all I could think to say. (I was still in the kitchen and, by the way, I still am. It turns out if you're a writer who starts out in the kitchen, you will always be there.)

This book has been very good to me. And here it is again. High on the list of self-indulgences, the novelist imagines the lives of her characters long after the book ends. Like God. Becca would be in her late fifties now; maybe she's a grandmother. Probably not. Perhaps Alexy is a third year associate in a large New York corporate law firm. Maybe Tory is working on a degree in public policy, after a few years in the Peace Corps in Central America. Christoph might be e-mailing Becca on some tips for making that Thanksgiving turkey since his wife won't be back from her business trip until late Wednesday night. These were the lives Becca and her friends rallied and petitioned for, not realizing what would be sacrificed in return. When I lived that life of women and children I had no idea we would be the last generation of women to do so. So Ulli might have been right, after all, when she said to Becca that, "This was the best life."

I heard those two women in my head for a long time, then one day they were gone. It's hard for me to remember the young mother who wrote that book, too; the little children who lived with me have flown the nest years ago. How wonderful, even if I can't, that at least Becca can be forever young.

Annette Williams Jaffee
Lumberville, Pa.
2000

The Author

Annette Williams Jaffee is the author of the novels *Recent History* (Putnam) and *The Dangerous Age* (Leapfrog Press). She lives in Bucks County, Pennsylvania, on the banks of the Delaware River where she is at work on a novel about the lives of writing women.

Also from Leapfrog Press
Annette Williams Jaffee's
The Dangerous Age

A wise and sensual tale about pursuing the one great passion of our lives, not in our youth, but at that last dangerous moment when everything we own and everyone we love is at risk.

The Millers are the envy of all who know them, a 'successful' couple on the verge of the best years of their lives. But a spate of recent deaths and the absence of her children, away at college, force Suzanne to confront the fact that her marriage is cold and empty.

When Suzanne meets Robert Parrish, a silver-haired banker from East Texas with a talent for real friendship with a woman and an appetite for sensual pleasure — suppressed for years in his own straight-laced marriage — she must decide between the secure life she chose after the shameful ending of a youthful love affair or the disdain of her children, the loss of friends and the financial uncertainty awaiting a woman who decides to uproot her life in pursuit of the true intimacy she has long denied herself.

With rare insight, keen social satire and some of the most touchingly rendered erotic scenes in recent memory, *The Dangerous Age* is above all a story about seizing ecstasy in our lives ... regardless of age, in spite of the consequences.

"Set aside a block of uninterrupted time to read Jaffee's new novel ... Her writing makes the reader feel everything, with the result being that this is a book that refuses to be put down. A touching and absorbing story that lingers long after the final page has been read; highly recommended."
                                        —*Library Journal* (**Starred Review**)

"It's pretty clear that Suzanne, the protagonist of Annette Williams Jaffee's third novel is entering *The Dangerous Age* ... Suzanne finds herself longing for a kind of romantic intensity she has never had. When she meets Robert ... they tumble into lust, and love ... She walks away from her entire life, takes and apartment and "lives for the night" ... How glorious to give oneself up to a great late-in-life passion."
                                        —*The New York Times Book Review*

"The pages turn themselves!"   —*Los Angeles Times Book Review*